Alveridgea

Alveridgea

&
THE LEGEND *of the* LONELY DOG

IVAN CLARKE
and
STU DUVAL

Atlantic Books
LONDON

To our grandchildren

A version of *Alveridgea* first published by Lonely Dog Print Ltd.
Original Almalogue concepts, images and words © Lonely Dog Ltd 2006.
All artworks are derived from Ivan Clarke's Lonely Dog Legacy Art Collection.
All rights reserved.

Lonely Dog and LD are the registered trademarks of Lonely Dog Ltd.

This edition first published in hardback and e-book in Great Britain in 2012 by
Atlantic Books, an imprint of Atlantic Books Ltd.

Copyright © Lonely Dog Ltd 2012

The moral right of Lonely Dog Ltd to be identified as the author
of this work has been asserted by them in accordance with the Copyright,
Designs and Patents Act of 1988.

1 2 3 4 5 6 7 8 9

A CIP catalogue record for this book is available from the British Library.

Hardback ISBN: 978 184887 332 2
E-book ISBN: 978 1 84887 334 6

Printed in Great Britain

Atlantic Books
An Imprint of Atlantic Books Ltd
Ormond House
26–27 Boswell Street
London
WC1N 3JZ

www.atlantic-books.co.uk

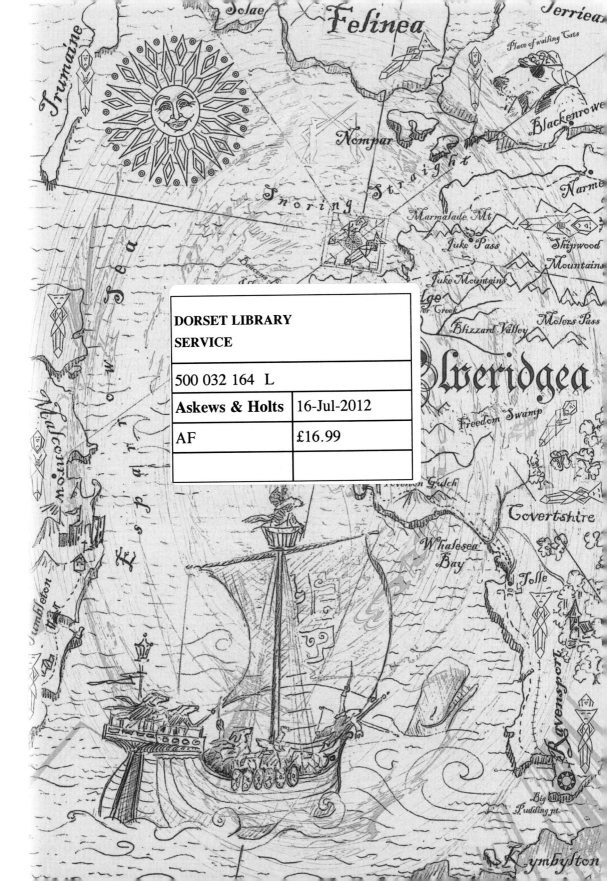

Prologue

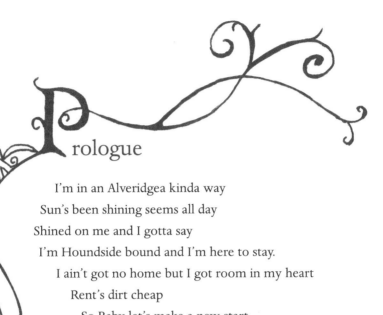

I'm in an Alveridgea kinda way
Sun's been shining seems all day
Shined on me and I gotta say
I'm Houndside bound and I'm here to stay.
I ain't got no home but I got room in my heart
Rent's dirt cheap
So Baby let's make a new start
In Port Alveridge
It'll be OK
'Cause I'm Houndside bound and I'm here to stay

—Missin' Tooth Memphis, *Blue Roots Anthology*

$\mathcal{S}$ecrets and legends. The land of Alveridgea abounds
with them. It is believed that every Houndling has a
guardian angel. It is also believed that every Houndling has a
destiny. All legends have beginnings and every Houndling's
story must start with the turning of the first page.

Tonight you can almost hear the rustle of this turning page, like a rush
of angels' wings. But the hushed words that begin this particular legend
go unheard as a tiny pup, asleep in a shoebox of Size 11 Tom Cat winkle-
pickers, is swept across a velvet sky, through cotton clouds and down
to a ribbon of silver on a satin sea. Blissfully unaware of the legend he
will become or of the tales that will be written of his exploits, the pup
snorts and wriggles as his guardian angel whisks him past the road that
leads from the purple-hued Juke Mountains and along the sparkling Juke
River, twisting and turning down to the coast. Tumbleroot and Cracklewood trees dapple the journey, affording glimpses of small hamlets and
fields ripe with honeysuckle wheat, laid out like a gloriously dishevelled

Port Alveridge Council Chambers, Viaduct Lane

quilt. Then the pair swoop in from the north, through gently rolling hills, over the bridge, and, finally, joyfully, into Port Alveridge.

The little town snuggles contentedly against the warm Esparrow Sea, protected from the cold winds that blow off the snow-capped Shipwoods to the east, splayed like a sleeping hound in the velvet darkness. It is a town like a pair of old jeans, scuffed and faded in all the right places. In a few hours, Port Alveridge will wake to the smell of the sea in its nose. Wilkers' boats, coal-fired clinkers captained by grizzled sea Hounds, will chug into port with cargo holds full of whale's milk, cream of the sea, ready to be fermented into frothy Wilks Beer. A flotilla of fishing boats will put out on to the Esparrow Sea in search of spotty russock, blubber-fin, butter wallop and one-eyed flappers the size of a fisherman's story, returning at dusk with nets straining and full.

As the evening sky begins to melt like butter in a skillet, Hounds will clamber from their boats and spill out of the huge brick Fish Cannery, heading for the bars and saloons along the Boulevard, which wraps round the wharf like a happy smile. Clapboard shacks with names like 'Rotten Catch', 'Houndwhistle Grill' and 'Marvo's Fine Dining and Auto Repair' sit cheek by jowl with solid brick establishments, tables littering the wide verandas, wrought-iron balconies ablaze with light. Here, a Hound can

Marvo's Bar
DOWNTOWN PORT ALVERIDGE

Sunday Fishing

sip a beer and fill his pipe with barley baccy as the air shimmers and hums with smoke and music. For, after dark, Port Alveridge is soaked in the blues. Old blues maestros like Missin' Tooth Memphis, Rusty Razor and the Snouts, and Stub Tail Tonks will open battered guitar cases and run fingers over yellowed piano keys.

But any Hound visiting the Port for the first time will sense something else, a smell so intense it rises above the smoky bar, over the heads of the sweaty worker Hounds. Mixed with the sweet scent of cellared wine is the Feline fragrance of ... Cats. For in Port Alveridge, unlike anywhere else in the land of Alveridgea, Cats and Hounds live side by side, separated only by the sparkling Juke River.

For now, the Juke River is flecked with starlight; morning is just around the corner, and the hills, the wharf, the streets, the ramshackle cabins, even the boats at anchor are asleep, snoring hoarsely like our Houndling, whimpering as he dreams, while the alleys and drowsy houses flash past. The flap of a page being turned is the only other sound to break the silence as the pair crest the hill and turn into the driveway of the old brick building that peers down at the town from the top of Tumbleton Avenue.

A peeling sign swings on squeaky hinges above a rusty wrought-iron gate: 'Alveridge County Orphanage'. It is a sprawling Hound-Gothic pile, built and rebuilt with new wings and additions, many of which, like the brick twin cupola, have left it looking less like an educational establishment and more like a sinking battleship. The Orphanage may have seen better days, but it has forgotten them entirely. A soft wind whispers tremulously on the stone, past windows ranged in uneven rows, shuttered and dark as a blind Hound's sockets. The old Cracklewood trees by the gate shiver together, loosening swirls of brittle leaves that spin in the pale-milk moonlight as our hero is set down on a step and the hand of his unseen guardian raps the great brass knocker and melts into the shadows.

Esparrow

Port **Alveridge**

Nautalis Beach

Whalesea Highway

Hotel Blackenrowe

Hotel Grande

Sunset Boulevard

Revellers Green

Revellers Point

Sunshine Point

Pie

Revellers Basin

Zotos

Tumbleton Ave

LeRoys

County Orphanage

Marvos Bo-Bos

Hotel Jupit

Rolleston Quay

Vernons Arms

Drawls End

Alveridge Town Hall

Beacons Street

Sunset Boulevard

Houndside

Telegraph Road

Hillcrest

Signal Road

South Telegraph Road

Old F

Hillcrest Stadium

Sth Alveridge

Sea

Gnarling Point

Lovers Leap

North Tolleston
Country Club

Raison Cove

North
Tolleston

Port Alveridge Fish Cannery

Pebble Bay

Catside

Minkas Cannery Mall

Catside
Orphanage

Viaduct

Tolleston Avenue

Viaduct Lane

P. A.
Stevedores

Monument bay

Tolleston Botanical

Basin

Petroleum company

Boat yards

Gardens

Fisherton

Port Alveridge
Council Chambers

Basin

Fisherton Docks

Old Whaling Station

Luke River

Alveridge Central
Railway Station

Alveridge Houndside

Veterans Home

Punters Rest
Golf Club

ton Road

Orchard Road

Fisherton

Sth Alveridge

Dingleton

Alveridge Power Station

CHAPTER I

The Houndling and the Guardian Angel

Git up off the porch, Mama, oh my, it jest can't be,
A lil' Hound in a worn ol' shoe – well, Lordy, Lordy me!

—Stompin' Stan Fiddler, *Clap Ya Ears on This!*, Side 2

'Rolph Flannegan, is that you? Do you have any idea what time it is?' a strident female voice growled in the darkness. 'You should be ashamed of yourself! What kind of example are you setting our Houndlings? Away with your Revellers down at the Green, drinking and carousing into the small hours!'

Bella Bostock, portly Matron of the Orphanage, threw open the door and stared out into the night. No one. She was about to go back indoors when she caught sight of the little bundle on the doorstep.

'Bless my snout! What is that?' She picked up the small rectangular object tied with string. 'It looks like a shoebox.'

If this was some Hound's idea of a joke there would be trouble. But as Bella began to untie the string, she felt something moving inside. And when she lifted the lid, her big eyes widened impossibly as she saw, cocooned in an old slipper and blinking in the yellow porch light at her startled face, a tiny Houndling!

'Lord have mercy! It's a poor wee Houndling!' she cried as she scooped him up into her generous bosom. She looked up into the starry night as if giving thanks to the heavens. 'How on earth did you get here?'

She turned inside just in time to see Rolph Flannegan coming down the stairs in his tattered nightgown, rubbing his eyes sleepily.

'Oh Rolph, did I wake you? And there I was thinking it was you stumbling home in the early hours.'

Rolph padded across the hallway to the front door and looked down at the shoebox. 'I'm sure it wasn't on the porch when I came home,' he rumbled, peering at the pup with far-away eyes.

Bella fairly glowed. 'Why, don't you see? The wind in the Cracklewood! The leaves swirling!'

The elderly Headmaster looked at her as if he was holding a knitting pattern upside down.

'It was a guardian angel!' she cried, as if stating the patently obvious. 'Swooshed down from the clouds above with this lonely little thing.'

Rolph Flannegan was about to suggest that a shoebox and old slipper were a strange means of conveyance for a guardian angel, but thought better of it. Like many folk, Bella still clung to her belief in a spiritual realm, and only the brave or the foolhardy would dare disabuse her. Especially in these hard times. Rolph tried to think of something else he might say, but before he had the chance Bella had bustled inside, pup clasped tight, leaving him scratching his snout.

The Houndling in the box bore no identification besides a terse note tied with string around his neck: 'Arthur Snout – No Next of Kin'.

'Poor little dear,' crooned Bella as she bathed and dressed him in a pair of oversized pyjamas. 'All alone in this big old world. Well, someone's been watching over you all right, given you a name and all.'

Rolph Flannegan decided that he might as well have himself a frothy nightcap before returning to bed. He sat down at the kitchen table, pulling on a frayed brown cardigan. Bella heaped Cracklewood on to the dying embers in the cast-iron range and soon a fire blazed, shedding a warm yellow glow over the room. The kitchen's shelves groaned with jars of jams and bottles of preserves. Well-scrubbed pots and pans hung from the rafters amid a flotilla of chequered tea towels, drying in the warm air. The old Headmaster watched Bella tend to the mysterious arrival from over the brim of his cup.

The Houndling giggled at the touch of Bella's hands. He had long, soft ears and hazelnut eyes and his little nose was black as a vicar's button. Yet he was unusually short, even for a pup.

'What kind of Houndling is this?' Rolph muttered. 'He looks all ears and snout if you ask me.'

'Well, sometimes good things come in small parcels.' Bella smiled knowingly. 'Anyway, there's always room for one more.'

The Headmaster shook his head as if unconvinced. The Orphanage was already packed to the rafters, and the

Rolph Flannegan

Executive Board had warned him not to take in any more strays. 'Fiscal responsibility' they had intoned. He drained his cup, yawned, then headed towards the stairs and his bedroom. Pausing by the kitchen door, he watched Bella tenderly comb the little Houndling's long russet ears. Arthur Snout looked back plaintively, his deep brown eyes seeming to seek acceptance in Rolph's grizzled face. A small smile danced around the pup's lips and a tiny pink tongue protruded playfully.

Bella stopped combing and took a long look at him. A quizzical expression crossed her face. 'You look somehow familiar…' she murmured, her voice trailing away like the steam from a kettle.

'I suppose we could find an extra bed,' Rolph mumbled, turning on his heel. 'Put him in the cot in Marvin's room.'

'I don't know…' Bella looked up, hesitant, at the mention of her son. 'Marvin always has an ear cocked, he needs his rest.'

Rolph snorted. Years ago when Bella had pleaded for a part-time position at the Orphanage, he had taken pity on her. Her husband, a mean-spirited drunkard, had died mysteriously at an illegal weasel fight, leaving her alone in the world with her young pup, Marvin. Bella had quickly proved an invaluable support. The orphan Houndlings adored her, and Rolph had come to rely on her, then totally depend on her to keep the Orphanage running.

In fact the dependence was mutual. Bella looked on the aged Headmaster as a father figure for her fractious son. The pup was surly and scheming and seemed to have inherited his father's temperament rather than his mother's heart. As the years progressed, Bella had dared to hope that her relationship with Rolph might turn into something more. She would send him come-hither looks after supper, when the Houndlings were tucked up in bed, but he would always briskly rebuff her. Recently, however, as Rolph peered at his increasingly grizzled reflection in the shaving mirror of a morning, he had begun to think that Bella's well-upholstered bosom might offer some comfort for a mature bachelor Hound like him.

'Put him in with Marvin. Who knows, it might be the making of the pup.'

Rolph climbed the stairs to the third floor. His bedroom was cluttered but orderly: a simple bed covered with an eclectic array of patchwork blankets, Bella's handiwork; bookshelves that sagged with academic tomes; a chipped porcelain sink with a cracked mirror; and a small wooden cabinet containing hair products, snout combs and musky after-shave colognes. One wall was hung almost end to end with sepia-tinted photographs of the bedroom's former occupants: severe-looking head-master Hounds with canes in their hands, furrowed brows and impressive academic snouts. All peering imperiously at the current headmaster as if ready to admonish him from their dusty frames.

The room's only nod to luxury was an overstuffed leather armchair. Rolph slumped gratefully into its comfy embrace. It was late and he was drained from the night's events. He was more than drained, he realized, as he caught sight of himself in the cracked mirror, he was *terrified*.

Earlier that dark evening, as he had stumbled up the hill overlooking the Port, he had felt a knocking in his chest, something more than just his ageing heart, pumping like a leaky piston, unused to such physical exertion. It was old secrets, banging on the door of his soul, demanding resurrection. When he reached the summit of the hill, gulping air like a drowning pup, he fell to his knees, loosening the collar of his sweat-drenched shirt.

For a long time he lay at the foot of an ancient Tumbleroot. He had lain here once before, he remembered, in a time long ago. A time when he was barely more than a pup, with no secrets to bury. He stroked the tree's roots like a lover's leg, and in the darkness remembered the sun spilling through dappled leaves, dancing on the silver frets of his guitar. A silhouette climbing the hill, her gypsy skirt flowing like spilt ink. He remembered her eyes, green as the Esparrow Sea, whitecaps dancing at the edges. They had laughed and sung that day, until the sun traded places with the moon and it was here, in the Tumbleroot's embrace, amid soft sea breezes, that they had lain that night. With the morning she was gone.

Roused from his memories, Old Rolph Flannegan shook his long, silvered ears and struggled to his feet. The moon was rising now, pale as a preacher's wife. Suddenly a blaze of light washed over him. The old Hound cautiously raised his head. Headlights! A black sedan was approaching the foot of the hill. He did not have to see the occupants to know exactly who they were. Tom Cats. And they were heading towards the farmhouse. In less than a minute the car would ford Cripplecat Creek. The elderly Hound began to stumble down the hill after the sedan. Tom Cats prowling the lonely roads of Houndside in the early hours could only mean some Feline malice.

By the time Rolph had lurched to the bottom of the hill, the black sedan had rolled to a stop by the barn. The purr of the engine died and the car seemed to crouch, leaking muddy water from the creek, exuding menace. The four doors opened silently and six Toms sidled out. Dressed in full-length leather coats, black as their hearts, they stood uncertainly, heads tilted to the breeze, sniffing the stink of Hound. For a sickening moment Rolph thought they had caught wind of him but they did not turn, moving stealthily towards the house where a solitary lamp glowed yellow in an open window. From within came the sound of gentle singing, a song unfamiliar to the Toms but one that Rolph recognized immediately, a cadence as warm as a first sip of Triple Malted Snarler, as old as childhood. A mother crooning to her pup.

> Hush lil' baby
>
> Hush your tears
>
> Mama's gonna stay all night right here
>
> Hush your whimperin'
>
> Hush your bark
>
> Mama's gonna stay right through the dark

Rolph opened his mouth to howl, but nothing came. He willed his legs to move, but they were rooted to the ground. All he could do was watch as the Toms first rolled an empty petrol drum to block the front door, then lashed the back door shut with a length of rusted chain and finally took up positions at each corner of the single-storey farmhouse.

> Hush lil' baby…

The stench of petrol filled the night air as the Toms stuffed rags into bottles they produced from under their coats.

Hush your tears…

They lit the wicks and watched the flames dance. The blazing bottles spiralled in the moonlight.

Momma's gonna stay all night right here.

The little farmhouse had stood at the end of the dirt lane for over a hundred years and its clapboards were as brittle as a dead cricket's skin. It did not burn, it imploded. The Toms retreated to their black sedan and watched impassively until the fireball diminished. Then they reversed back down the rutted lane, the dust raised by their tyres mingling with the smoke from the crackling blaze. The singing had stopped. Rolph Flannegan finally found his voice. A yowl, ripped from his very soul, was lost in the roar of the departing sedan.

Reaching under the armchair the old Headmaster retrieved a bottle of Triple Malt and a glass tumbler. He splashed himself a slug of whisky, but his hand was shaking so much he couldn't drink it. The glass slipped from his grip and shattered on the floor. He waited for Bella's inquisitorial call, but she was too busy with the new Houndling. Rolph reached for a dustpan and broom. He hated mess. All his life he had endeavoured to eliminate it, to keep things neat and tidy, have a cubby-hole for every situation. But now as his shaking hands swept the broken glass, he recognized, with mounting trepidation, that his well-ordered life had become very messy indeed.

At a sudden knock on the door, Rolph snapped out of his reveries and hurriedly stuffed the whisky bottle under his mortarboard.

'Headmaster.'

It was Bella.

'I've just put the little one to bed and I'm off there myself.' Her voice dropped huskily. 'Is there anything else you might be needing tonight?'

On the other side of the closed door, Rolph feigned deep snoring, which he continued until he heard Bella's heavy, slippered feet depart down the corridor and her bedroom door close with a resigned thud.

Marvin Bostock turned to the Houndling asleep in the bed next to his, peering at the new arrival with a disgruntled scowl.

'I'm not supposed to be sharing my room with strays. You should be out in the dorm with the other orphans.' He glowered at the sleeping pup with the long, soft ears and large snout, then poked him spitefully. 'You don't even look like a Hound, and you stink like a Cat.' Another painful poke.

Arthur awoke, tears welling up in his big brown eyes, and began to whimper. Bella's footsteps came scurrying down the corridor.

'What's the matter my wee lonely dog?' she cooed, opening the door.

Marvin hid beneath his sheets, pretending to sleep, a malicious smile on his lips.

'*What's the matter wee lonely dog?*' he mimicked under his breath. 'Cat got your tongue?'

CHAPTER II

The Protest Movement and Cannery Fire

They say them
Four chimneys
Reach way up to the stars,
I say them
Four smokestacks
Look more like prison bars!

—Van Trong, *Protest Songs To Dance To*, vol. 7

*H*aving settled her newest foundling in Marvin's room, Bella Bostock crept away, yawning. One more hungry snout to feed, but they would manage somehow. There would be time to think about it tomorrow. 'There's been enough excitement for one night,' she thought – but the thought was interrupted by the rusty clang of the doorbell.

As she indignantly wondered who could be calling at such an hour, it rang again. Fearful that the din would wake every Houndling in the building, she quickly padded downstairs and unlocked the great wooden door. Peering suspiciously outside, she half expected to find another foundling. Instead, her eyes met the unsteady gaze of the kneeling Baron of Beaconsfield.

The Baron belched twice and wavered unsteadily to his feet, wheezing like a leaky accordion. He had once been a Hound of erect carriage and noble bearing, but in old age it was as though the carriage had been derailed, damaging its grand facade. He was wearing a tattered military overcoat pinned with ribbons as faded as his eyesight.

'Is that you, Baron?' she demanded rather than asked. Then, without waiting for an answer, 'Have you been drinking?'

The Baron stifled another belch and gripped the railing for support.

'Just a drop... or two. Is the good Headmaster available?'

Bella peered over her bosom like a judge summing up from the bench.

'He is neither good nor available! Every Hound in the place is fast asleep.' Her face softened, in the manner of an overripe lemon.

Bella was accustomed to the Baron's visits, unannounced, and usually when most decent Hounds-folk were home in bed. His chauffeur would drive him the winding journey from his isolated baronial estate for a night playing cards and reminiscing with old comrades and war veterans. The Headmaster could always be counted on for a couch to sleep on, somewhere inside the rambling Orphanage.

'Has he heard', the Baron's growl was deadly serious, 'about the Cannery?'

'The Cannery? There'll be time for talk of workers' rights in the morning, Baron. Now, if you'll—'

Bella Bostock stopped, and stared over the Baron's shoulder to a molten glow, a ball of liquid flame raging where the Port Alveridge Fish Cannery stood. She turned in panic to go and fetch the Headmaster but Rolph Flannegan was already creaking down the stairs to join them. The three Hounds stood on the porch, staring in disbelief. The Cannery was ablaze.

For more than two hundred years, Port Alveridge had been domi-
nated by the hulking factory of blackened brick that squatted on a
peninsula thrust out from the waterfront into the Esparrow Sea. Generations of Hounds had toiled in the Cannery's gloomy maze of cavernous
warehouses and grimy machine shops. Still more laboured in the factory
itself, a glowering cathedral of rusty iron girders and filthy windows,
filled with the deafening racket of the steam-powered machinery used to
process the fish that slithered along the production lines.

Even now, from their distant vantage point at the top of Tumbleton
Avenue, the three shocked Hounds could see the Cannery's four enormous chimneys rising above the flames. Every Hound in Port Alveridge
complained about the chimneys, about the stench and
noise and smoke belching night and day, but the
pollution was only half the story – the Cannery
chimneys were also a visual reminder of happier
times long lost. A time before Cats.

For though Port Alveridge is a town unique
in Alveridgea, where Cats and Hounds live
side by side, they do not live as equals. The
ramshackle sprawl of Houndside is lively
and chaotic, a warren of shacks where
labourers and dockers reside, builders
and plumbers and thousands of Cannery workers. But on the other bank
of the Juke River is a wholly different
world.

Common Alveridgean Snufflebeak
(NOTED NUISANCE)

Catside nestles on the warm side of the hill overlooking the town. Up here, gentle ocean breezes caress meticulously manicured hedges and great swathes of carefully cultivated lawn. Here, deep within beautiful groves of Cottonball trees, shady and cool, are the white stucco mansions and stately homes of the moneyed Cats, their interiors adorned with luxurious shagpile carpets, lavish damask curtains and sparkling chandeliers of pure Felinean crystal.

It was not always so. The Port Alveridge Fish Cannery was built by Hounds for Hounds two centuries ago, during the Golden Age of trade. They had shipped canned spotty russock by the boatload north to Felinea and upon these profits the Port had grown and blossomed. But now, no landmark in all of Port Alveridge more bitterly represented the abject subjugation of the Hounds. They had squandered the profits of the factory as only Hounds can and in more recent years the Cats had taken over. Cats now controlled every aspect of its lucrative production and wallowed in the wealth it brought them. None more so than Colonel A. K. Ruddegan, Mayor of Port Alveridge and now president of the Cannery.

'How did it happen?' Rolph rumbled.

'No one knows. But it's worse…' the Baron stammered, 'worse than you can imagine… Van Trong is dead.'

He stared in horror as the night sky blazed red, the four chimneys of the Cannery towering above the flames like martyrs at the stake, the fishing fleet cowered in the docks at their feet.

'Van Trong?' Rolph's gruff voice faded to a whimper. 'Dead?'

Even Bella, who kept her snout out of politics, shook her head vehemently. Van Trong, the Working Hounds' Troubadour, Minstrel to the Masses. How was such a thing possible?

But Rolph's whimper had already become a howl and, as it was carried on the great plumes of smoke swirling through the town's streets, it insinuated its way into every house in Port Alveridge, seeping under bolted doors, creeping down chimney pots, up threadbare stairs and along darkened alleyways. Soon all of Houndside would know the horrible truth.

'His wife and baby too,' the Baron said. 'But that's not the worst… They're saying he did it. They're saying it was Van Trong himself that started the fire.'

'I don't believe it.' Rolph Flannegan shook his white whiskers angrily. 'I won't believe it.'

'Ruddegan says he has evidence…'

'Ruddegan?' the Headmaster barked. 'Bloody duplicitous Cats!'

'You'll watch your tongue around my wee Houndlings!' Bella snapped like a rat trap, then remembered her charges were all asleep.

By morning, Rolph Flannegan's anguished howl of disbelief would be echoed in every dusty boulevard and decrepit alley in Houndside. For if the Cannery was a symbol of Houndish oppression, Van Trong had been the lone roar of defiance, the one figure capable of galvanizing his fellow Hounds.

Van Trong had sprung from the obscurity of a small farm in Cripplecat Creek to take on the might of Mayor Ruddegan and the Cat Conglomerates. Short but dashing in his trademark long black coat and tilted fedora,

Van Trong was a Hound who commanded attention. He had formed a Cannery Workers Union and urged browbeaten Hounds to join, only to find that years of oppression had sapped their spirit. 'You can't change nuthin'!' they told him.

But Van Trong had not given up. When his rhetoric failed, he'd picked up his guitar, for he knew that as surely as the sun rises hot and fast, the way to a Hound's heart is through music. Music raw and loud, twanged and strummed and stomped: full-throated, heart-pounding music! Songs of misery relieved, of love won and lost, of Hounds of old; songs to ease the daily grind.

When Van Trong played his five-string Alveridgean guitar, Hounds stopped and listened. His songs raged against inequality and prejudice, and brought Hounds flocking to Union meetings, stirring them and igniting their desire to fight. Van Trong didn't just sing the blues, he bled them. They said his guitar was strung with barbed wire, his music cut so deep. When he sang 'It Just Ain't Right', a fire began to smoulder in even the weariest Hound's eyes and all the Hounds of Port Alveridge joined the rallying cry:

> Boss Man you can beat me, you can even dock my pay
> But Boss Man you get ready 'cause here comes Judgement Day
> It just ain't right
> It just ain't right
> I'm gonna stand up and fight
> 'Cause it just ain't right!

For months, A. K. Ruddegan had been watching through the plate-glass windows of his seventh-floor factory office as, slowly at first, then in an unstoppable torrent, the Cannery Workers Union swelled and the roar of protest grew deafening.

Diminutive in stature but a giant in avarice, Mayor Ruddegan had eyes of cold obsidian and a moustache as thin as a cut-throat razor. He cared little that the work in his Cannery was back-breaking, the pay pitiable, the hours torturously long. He cared only that in a town where jobs were scarce, every Hound on the steaming, clattering production line was thankful for the work. More than thankful: they were utterly dependent.

He had watched, then waited, as productivity fell, profits began to ebb, and the other Fat Cats of the Conglomerate began to panic. Then he told them his plan.

On the evening of the fire, hundreds of Union Hounds joined Van Trong in yet another protest at the Cannery, torchlight flickering in their fervent eyes. Standing on an improvised crate-box stage, the troubadour gave his finest performance, his husky voice soaring, his beloved guitar oozing the blues.

Ruddegan gazed down at the angry crowd from the comfort of his richly upholstered scarlet leather armchair. He plucked a goldfish from a cut-crystal bowl on his desk and held it momentarily by the tail, observed the gasping mouth, the bulging eyes, then swallowed it whole and smiled, revealing his perfect, glittering incisors.

As Van Trong began to sing 'It Just Ain't Right!', Ruddegan stared down from his office window and signalled to one of his thugs standing in the shadows behind the protestors.

The Hounds yowled in chorus: 'Boss Man you get ready 'cause here comes Judgement Day' as they waved their flaming torches high in the night sky. Ruddegan looked on, tapping his foot in time with the chorus as if counting down. Behind the scene, his thugs busied themselves. There was a sudden flare then a dull explosion that illuminated the towering chimneys of the Cannery like a flash of lightning. Panicked hounds fled the mayhem. Waiting Toms turned and closed the huge security gates, cordoning off the area. Van Trong had not left the blaze. As Ruddegan looked on from a distance he took a long draw on his cigar. 'It just ain't right!' he sneered quietly as he blew a long plume of smoke across the room.

ROLPH FLANNEGAN

Rolph Flannegan still lives in the old red-bricked building that housed the Alveridge County Orphanage. Even now, it remains impressive, in a Gothic style, despite its current forlorn condition. The orphans have long since vacated the dormitories and the tired old schoolroom hasn't heard a houndling's laughter in many years. Not that much laughing went on during the lessons there anyway. Rolph was always a strict disciplinarian, Now, in the late autumn of his years, he still administers his life with punctuality and order, that you would expect of a retired schoolmaster. His residence is in one small corner of the rambling building, where he is, and always has been, a confirmed and committed bachelor. This is apparent in everything about him, his dress, and in his modest abode as well. The décor, although slightly shabby and worn, has a distinctive masculine appearance. The book-shelves are well stocked, mostly classic yarns, motorcycle manuals and Alveridgean history books. The antique refrigerator in the compact kitchen is also well stocked with neat rows of Speckled Wilks beer, one of his unpresumptuous luxuries. His lounge is cosy, not large, and is eminently set up for the simple style of life a hound of Rolph's years can enjoy. A pipe of snuffle-baccy to smoke, an overstuffed sofa to snooze on, and a gramophone tucked away in the corner to play his impressive collection of Blues music. The walls are crammed with dusty images and sepia photographs of his past glories. School outings in the old orphanage bus, Bella and Rose - the adored Orphanage aunties and Rolph him-self in a severe black mortar and academic gown. He often lingers by these captured memories when he is in a nostalgic frame of mind. To see him chuckling to him-self at a memory or event encapsulated in one of the many photographs would seem to contradict the image that most people in Port Alveridge hold of crusty old Rolph Flannegan.

To see him holding forth, in his tattered beige cardy, down at his favourite watering hole, Marvo's Bar and Grill, is to see a feisty octogenarian pounding the table, demanding that all who hear him "should mark my words!" For it is here, at Marvo's, that Rolph, and his equally aged and equally bellicose buddy, The Baron of Beaconsfield, hold court. Their table at the back of the bar is ritually reserved and from it they survey what they rightly believe to be their fiefdom. The years have brought sweep-ing changes to Port Alveridge, but not to Rolph

Flannegan and those he considers privileged enough to share his table, and most evenings, his bile. This vitriol is mostly aimed at the new breed of cat that has flouted old Rolph's sensibilities and the generation that bore him. He is at his best, snout thrust forward, eyes a-sparkle, when he is remonstrating about the way things have changed, and what should be done to rectify them. The old headmaster in him never retired, just got a bit grey in the muzzle. His dire predictions and thumping oratory have earned him a begrudging respect from the older regulars at Marvo's, although the younger hounds, in afros and flares, look upon him as a cranky reminder of their own unfortunate school days and the slightly barmy masters that caned and berated them. However, give him a few pints of Wilkes and his mood will change, usually corresponding directly to the number of hounds gathered around his table, and also to the number of empty beer jugs at his elbow. Rolph will then spin tales of the orphanage, and, in particular, his early influence in the life of Arthur Snout, aka Lonely Dog. He never tires of telling it, although the audience sometimes tires of hearing it. How, according to Rolph, he personally encouraged, nay, tutored the young Arthur Snout in the manly art of playing the five-string Alveridgean Guitar. "His first chords were the ones I taught him! Now that's an umbilical cord that can't be broken! He plays guitar now exactly as I showed him then." Now guitar playing was, to be truthful, one of old Rolph's fortes. He could, and still does, pick a mean blues riff and his Houndskittle jams down on the Revellers Green are still remembered. Yet this was not something that he wanted made

public. In fact all through his life, he had tried hard to conceal the other, opposite, side of his rather fusty personality. In short he was a stern schoolmaster by day... and a free-spirited troubadour by night. Carefully replacing his black mortar board for a red bandana, he would slip out of the orphanage and onto his beloved Houndster V2 Whizzer, guitar stowed in the sidecar, and burn a blukie down Tumbleton Ave to Revellers Green. There he'd hang out with all the other wild free-spirited artistes, strumming and jamming into the warm summer nights beneath a huge Tumbleroot tree. Then, when he had his fill of music and Wilkes, he would somehow manoeuvre his houndster back up Tumbleton Ave. Once home, he'd return to form and carefully wash and rinse his sweaty bandana and hang it to dry amongst the orphanage tea-towels in the hot-water cupboard. Thus his secret had been much like his bandana, hidden in the closet. Yet the door of that closet had been forced open by a little lonely hound with a passion for music that matched his own... The patrons of Marvo's have all gone home now, leaving the old headmaster to his beer dregs and his thoughts. Then, with just one lone bar hound for an audience, Rolph Flannegan picks up his beloved guitar and begins to sing...

CHAPTER III

Houndside County Orphanage

All Orphan Houndlings should be fed thrice a day, bathed once a week, and caned as often as deemed necessary, in strict accordance with the rules of this Honourable Establishment.

— *The Headmaster's Regulatory Manual*,
vol. CLXVIII, p.6899

*I*n the nine years since his arrival at the Orphanage as
a Houndling in a shoebox, Arthur Snout had climbed every
Cracklewood tree that graced the grounds of his home. He had
swung from their branches in spring, slept in their shade in
summer and bounded through their falling leaves as winter
began to draw in. They had stood for as long as he had been
there; they had stood for two hundred winters before that. Now
some were being cut down for firewood. If times had been
tough when Arthur Snout arrived, they were even tougher now.

With a sickening crack and a groan like a dying whale, the trees crashed
to the ground one by one. The old Cracklewoods were needed as fuel to
stoke the ancient boiler. Without them the orphans would freeze. Rolph
watched the last tree tumble and with it went his spirit, each tree a repre-
sentation of fallen hopes and broken dreams. He turned up the collar
of his threadbare coat and shuffled morosely back indoors, his eyes as
lifeless as the dead branches in the snow.

View Towards the Cannery, Port Alveridge

Bella had a cup of steaming hot coffee waiting for him in the kitchen, but he ignored it, and her, and slowly climbed the stairs to his room. He would need something much stronger to deal with the deep and gripping pain he felt, tight as a towel in a wringer. He stood at the window looking past the felled Cracklewoods, down to the Port and the Cannery chimneys standing stark on the horizon, belching smoke into the reddening sky as the sun sank into the Esparrow Sea.

In the decade since the fateful night on which Van Trong and fifty-three Union Hounds had perished in the fire, the factory had risen from its ashes. The official investigation into the blaze concluded that the fire had been an act of arson. A. K. Ruddegan docked the wages of every Hound on the payroll and sued the Cannery Workers Union for the money needed to – as he pointedly put it – 'rebuild their future'. Beaten, betrayed and facing the bleak prospect of generations of unemployment, the Hounds of the Port had sacrificed what little they still had to secure their positions, only to discover, when they lined up to reapply for their jobs, that as part of the refurbishment Ruddegan had automated much of the plant. They were now 'surplus to requirements'. A thousand more Hounds were suddenly without work, discarded like undersized fish. It was then that the Great Exodus began.

Disillusioned with a struggle that had left them with nothing, the few remaining Union Hounds quit the Port with their families and headed east to the Juke Mountains to set up a community free of Cat influence. They were quickly followed by other Cannery Hounds, whose dilapidated pick-ups, piled high with all their earthly possessions, rattled over

Catnip and Canapes

dirt roads towards the Jukes and further east still to the distant Shipwood Mountains, a remote haven of Houndish isolationists and Moonshiners.

Rolph lost many a good Houndskiffle buddy to the Great Exodus.

'Soon it'll be just you and me, Flannegan,' the Baron would bark on his increasingly infrequent visits.

The Port of Alveridge, now glowing in the dying sun, felt to Rolph as if its heart had been ripped out. The remaining folk still went about their work, but it was as though their spirit had decamped to the mountains in the back of the rusty pick-ups with the other Hounds. Slowly, like a winter shadow, Conglomerates from Catside and even as far afield as Felinea were creeping over Houndside, snapping up empty houses and tenements at rock-bottom prices and taking over struggling Hound businesses for criminally small sums. Rolph himself had had several offers from Feline entrepreneurs for the Orphanage, whose crumbling Gothic majesty and hilltop location would make the perfect site for a Cat Casino and Luxury Hotel. He always told them bluntly where to stick their Fat Cat chequebooks, but the truth was that the Orphanage was in dire straits. The Board no longer had money enough to pay his wages, let alone to clothe and feed the orphans. It was all too much.

Rolph was about to turn away from the dismal view when he noticed movement amongst the toppled Cracklewoods. It was Arthur Snout. Rolph watched as the little Hound stroked the felled trees tenderly, like dying loved ones. Lonely – even Rolph now thought of Arthur Snout as Lonely Dog – Lonely was a strange one all right, the old Headmaster mused. That very morning, when the sawyer had arrived and was about to swing his axe into the first Cracklewood, there had come a lone voice from high up in the branches: 'It just isn't right!' It was Lonely!

Rolph had first cajoled, then threatened the little mutt in order to get him to come out of the tree, but Lonely had refused to climb down. Even Bella's sweet-talking hadn't worked. Finally Bronson, the eldest of the orphans, as big as a brick bungalow and with a heart to match, had climbed up to join Arthur, eventually gently talking him down. 'It still ain't right!' the young Hound had kept on whispering.

The little Hound had always been full of surprises, the Headmaster reminded himself, and astonishing resilience. Rolph knew better than anyone that Arthur's early years at the Orphanage had been hard. At Marvin's malicious instigation, Arthur's fellow orphans had taken to calling him Lonely Dog, and even Rolph had to agree that the name suited the little pup perfectly. It hadn't taken long for the other Hounds to realize that he was different in all sorts of ways – un-Houndly ways. Arthur Snout was short for a start, his snout was too long, his legs too stubby. True, this wasn't so odd in itself – other Hounds were short and snoutish – but Arthur Snout didn't *act* like a Hound.

By nature, Hounds are gregarious and tribal, never happier than when in a pack. Yet Lonely didn't seem to feel any of that primal urge to be part of the group, to run with the Houndlings: he was that highly unusual specimen – a private Hound. Not that Arthur considered himself a loner. Rather, he just preferred to be alone.

It was hardly surprising that in those early years Arthur had made few friends. But there was one important exception: a Houndette with brown button eyes, a butter-coloured snout and long ears tied like pigtails. Kelzie arrived two years after Lonely. She was shy to the point of tears, preferring to retreat into her own little world, which Rolph surmised was why she and Lonely had become friends. They were kindred souls.

There was also the matter of Arthur's deeply un-Houndish clothes. Whereas Hounds are by nature scruffy, adopting a casually dishevelled look, Lonely favoured clothes that were dapper, tailored, refined – almost Cat-like. His sartorial sense was the result of a chance discovery in the Orphanage attic, where, amid musty blankets and tatty, outdated schoolbooks, Lonely had found Rolph's old wind-up gramophone and a stack of scratched discs. Arthur was drawn to the crackle and static of this once popular music, playing the records over and over, thrilling to singers half of Houndside had forgotten: Memphis Two Fingers, Tootin' Joe Boottapper, Rusty Razor and the Snouts! But among former heroes of Houndskiffle, one stood snout and shoulders above the rest: a blues guitarist named Van Trong who wore a long black coat and tilted fedora. Gradually, to everyone's bemusement, Lonely had begun to acquire clothes that matched Van Trong's look: a long black coat with buttoned cuffs and tails; a white shirt and string tie; a dented old fedora given to him by the Baron. Arthur even took the time to shine his shoes to the glossy patina he saw in Van Trong's photo.

Rolph had tried to discourage this affectation, fearing the other Hounds would bully Lonely. Bella had tried too. But the little Hound had a surprisingly stubborn streak. Despite being the butt of endless jokes, he would not be deterred.

Most unusual of all, to the Headmaster's mind, were Lonely's nocturnal music practices. One night, creeping back into the Orphanage, high on Houndskiffle and ale, Rolph had heard strange sounds coming from the music room. Peeping round the door, he had been startled to see young Lonely sitting cross-legged on the floor with an old Trumaine seven-and-a-half-string in his lap.

Arthur had not been taught the intricate fingering needed to make that difficult instrument sing, but there he was, eyes closed, fingers moving nimbly over the frets like he was born to it. Rolph watched as Lonely began to pick out a simple melody in 7/4 beat. He looked on with amazement as the little Hound struggled to his feet and, though dwarfed by the huge guitar, lifted his head to the ceiling… and began to sing.

His voice was unlike anything the Headmaster had heard before. Soft, so soft there was no fear it would wake the Orphanage, but not angelic, no, not at all. His voice was as sharp as barbed wire – rusty barbed wire, twanging in the rain. But there was something else: the song wasn't a cover version of the old tracks he listened to in the attic, but some-thing Lonely had clearly written himself, something about him, Rolph Flannegan.

> Old Rolph got eyes that shine like a shoe
>
> De da do dah dumbly doo
>
> If old Rolph had a penny he'd give it you
>
> De da do dah dumbly doo
>
> Someday I wanna be just like you
>
> Old Rolph I do de dumbly doo

Rolph had never heard a young Houndling sing with such a voice. He stood for a long while simply listening. The words caught him by surprise. Was this just any old rhyme or did the little Hound really feel this way? Rolph coughed politely. Lonely stopped singing, opened his eyes and looked up in horror, the Trumaine dropping to the floor.

But when it came, Rolph's voice had been gentle, even fatherly.

'Way past your bedtime, Arthur Snout. You best run off to your dorm now.'

Watching Lonely stroke the fallen Cracklewood trees, the old Head-master, his lips wet with whisky, remembered that night, that song, and slumped into his study chair, and thought of old sins.

Downstairs, Lonely came in from the grounds carrying an unwieldy armful of wood for Bella's fire. The kitchen was empty and Arthur stopped and revelled in the homely comfort of the dilapidated room, breathing in the delectable aroma of pea and meatball soup, warming himself in the glow.

He would have been surprised to hear his headmaster's thoughts for, in spite of the rough and tumble, the bullying and his solitary ways, Arthur Snout felt quite at home in the rickety, sprawling Orphanage. He was no longer intimidated by the vast Gothic pile with its rambling corridors of panelled doors and warren of dusty rooms. He had no prob-lem drifting off to sleep in the dark dormitory with its wire-sprung beds and rag-stuffed pillows, and he even enjoyed the clamour of the rowdy dining hall, seated at one of the long tables carved with the names of every orphan who had eaten there, beneath the framed portraits of headmasters and prefects past. Most of all Lonely loved the Orphanage grounds, overgrown and wild, with Tumbleroot and Cracklewood trees to climb, dense copses of Knick-knack bushes where a Houndling could build huts, and muddy creeks on which he might float a shoe-boat.

Dashing back into the kitchen, fearful her soup was boiling over, Bella saw Lonely standing, dreaming, still clutching his armful of wood.

'My! Aren't you the thoughtful little gentleman!' she cooed, planting a wet kiss on his oversized snout. 'Here, have one of my GingerCat biscuits, straight out of the oven they are. And I've let down the cuffs on your suit trousers, now that you've grown a bit more.'

It was at just this moment that Marvin, trailing Lonely and bent on some mischief, or perhaps simply drawn by the scent of freshly baked biscuits, appeared in the doorway.

'See what young Arthur has brought me?' Bella said to her son. 'He's such a helpful little Hound.'

'I was just coming to ask if you needed wood,' Marvin fibbed effortlessly. His head was bowed, voice quavering as though upset, but his eyes were blazing with anger and jealousy.

'Were you, my little Houndling?' Bella stroked Marvin's ears. 'You're such a good boy. Here, have a GingerCat.'

She passed her son the biscuit she had been holding, temporarily forgetting Lonely, who stood empty handed. Arthur turned and went back out to the fallen trees.

Marvin felt a small surge of victory. He was increasingly resentful of his mother's evident affection for the ridiculously dressed usurper. Why could she not see that this pathetic foundling had ruined everything? Even Rolph seemed to be taken in. Many a time Marvin had caught the old Headmaster staring at Lonely with obvious warmth, with something almost like pride in his rheumy eyes. Marvin's jealousy had festered now for years and was made all the worse because Lonely treated him with the same cheerful good humour he did the other Houndlings. This strange-looking creature that had suddenly appeared in their midst was threatening his top-dog status! And so he focused all his malice, all his cruel jokes, and all his anger on Lonely.

The other Hounds, though they sometimes joined in with Marvin's pranks and bullying, bore Lonely no real ill will. They could not know that Marvin's aim was to chase the little Houndling out of the Orphanage and out of his life. To them, this kind of behaviour was simply a fact of Orphanage life. Houndlings bullied each other, and were bullied themselves: their boundless energy spilled over and they lashed out. It was all just high jinks, as long as no one got hurt too badly. Better to ask for forgiveness than permission was their motto. Besides, Rolph was usually on hand to cane sense into any Houndling who went too far.

But, as Marvin had noticed, Rolph seemed increasingly preoccupied these days. The grey on his snout now bloomed like a field of snow grass and as he grew long in the tooth so his attention span grew shorter. He could often

Young Marvin

be found staring into the distance, lost in his thoughts and secrets, while behind him the Hounds made the most of his distractedness, taking the opportunity to fool around.

Storming up the stairs to quieten the bedlam, Bella would find Houndlings swinging from ceiling fans, setting each other's tails alight with Bunsen burners, drawing chalk pictures that would make a sailor Hound blush, while Rolph stood looking out of the window, oblivious to the mayhem around him.

These classroom riots provided ample opportunity for Marvin to rid himself of Lonely once and for all. He would probably have been

Cruisin'

successful but for the eldest orphan, Bronson, who often sprang to Arthur's defence. The Orphanage Hounds – including Marvin – had long ago learned to respect the older Hound, who stood head and shoulders over them with his imposing physique, square snout and arms like axles. He affected the style of the biker Hounds whose posters adorned his wall: ears tied back behind his head, a studded leather waistcoat, and a pair of old spectacles he'd found, painted black to look like biker-shades. Bronson had developed a habit of sneaking off at night and hanging out with the real bikers, playing pool and listening to their tales of bluster and bravado. He spoke in a low rumble, like a throbbing Houndster twin-carb. A quiet growl from Bronson was all it took for the younger Houndlings to retreat and find some other means of releasing their pent-up energy.

More often than not, Lonely would leave the Houndlings to their japery and rowdy shenanigans and escape to the music room at the rear of the Orphanage. Here he would paw the worn instruments and pluck at the strings on Rolph's guitars, which the Headmaster had acquired from a sale at a music emporium down on the wharf. Sometimes, though Lonely did not know this, Bronson would sit outside the closed music room door and listen to the keening blues. In Lonely's silent stoicism, his unfailing optimism, Bronson saw something of himself; for his part, little Arthur thought of Bronson as a big brother, a mentor, and his friend.

By rights Bronson should already have left the Orphanage. The rules stated that at fifteen years of age any Hound could take up an apprentice-ship down at the docks. However, Bronson had become indispensable: to Rolph he was the Orphanage's unofficial enforcer, keeping the young

Houndlings in line with a snarl or a clip over the ears; to Bella he was the gentle giant who could open jam jars, fix the radiator and tend to all her other mechanical troubles; to the orphans he was the big brother they all wished they had. But to Marvin, Bronson was a brick wall, the wall that thwarted his plans to be rid of Lonely Dog.

Bronson had been quick to notice that Marvin's cruellest pranks and most hurtful bullying were focused on Lonely; he had seen Arthur's bruises and welts in the Orphanage showers and did not need to ask how he had come by them. Finally, Bronson had had enough. He waited until it was just him and Marvin, alone, in the bathroom. With one huge hand, he pinned the Houndling to the wall.

'You wanna pick on someone? Pick on me. 'Cause if I find even a scratch on Arthur Snout again I'm gonna knot your tail like a string of beads!'

And so Marvin plotted Lonely's downfall in secret and bided his time, much as the black-snoutbiter spider patiently waits for its opportunity to strike. The moment would have to be right, and the action profound. Marvin wanted Lonely gone, and gone for good. No more of this little Houndling usurper charming his way into what was rightfully his.

CHAPTER IV

························

The Forbidden Shed and the Greasy Tarpaulin

Oh the sea is so cruel, and the wind cuts like a knife
And sweethearts and lovers they only cause strife
For only one thing is true and won't surely part
A five-string guitar and one broken heart

— R. Flannegan, *Green Houndskiffle Blues,*
The Underground Recordings

*O*ld Rolph pulled his crumpled red bandana from its hiding place among the pages of his hefty volume of *Latin Verb Conjugations*. It was time for his weekly clandestine excursion to Revellers Green. He wore the same bandana every week, discreetly washing it and secreting it among the tea towels in the kitchen hot-water cupboard to dry. This, along with the five-string guitar that he concealed in the old woodshed out the back, represented the flipside of his straight-laced academic life as an orphanage headmaster. For the life he fastidiously kept hidden from view, screened from Bella and the Orphanage Board, was the free-wheeling life of a Reveller – an acoustic Hound!

It was a life that old Rolph lived with furtive exhilaration. His abiding, secret passion was Houndskiffle – the raw, unvarnished rhythm of Old Port Alveridge: acoustic heaven. His heroes were Hounds from the other side of life's tracks, Hounds like Memphis Two Fingers and Vinegar Bob, Hounds with rhythm in their souls and songs that leaked blue all over their guitars, always one string away from the law and one song away from fame.

Once a week Rolph would trade his rigid black mortarboard for his red knotted bandana and steal away into the night to drink jugs of Wilks and stomp and jam, to forget calculus and chalk-boards and simply skiffle into the small hours. The terms of his appointment did not allow for such un-headmasterly conduct; such ribald shenanigans would make his employment untenable. Which is why he went to great pains to hide his weekly jaunts to the Green from the puritan Orphanage Board. And from Bella, who would definitely turn off the tap of her affection if she got wind of his Bohemian alter-ego. And so, once back within the confines of the Orphanage, Rolph hid his Revelling paraphernalia and reprised his role as the grim-snouted, no-nonsense headmaster and crusty academic role-model.

On this summer's evening, the Houndlings were safely asleep in their dorms and Bella had gone to bed, her tail in curlers. Rolph crept out, heading for the old woodshed at the back of the Orphanage. Once his eyes had adjusted to the gloom, he walked softly behind the shed and lifted up a greasy tarpaulin to reveal a gleaming two-cylinder Houndster Whizzer, complete with woven-cane sidecar and brass headlamp. It was Rolph's pride and joy, one he and Bronson had spent many furtive evenings restoring.

The rusted old Whizzer had been a present from the Baron. 'Had it in my army days, 1st Houndsford Bike Artillery. Why not give that Bronson lad a crack at getting it going again? But for heaven's sake, don't tell Bella. She'll pickle your ears, Flannegan, and mine as well!'

Rolph wheeled the Whizzer quietly down Tumbleton Avenue until it was safe to kick the old bike into life without waking half the Orphanage. The engine erupted with a sound like a dozen Cats in a cement mixer, then spluttered off down the street, trailing a noxious cloud of blue smoke. Rakishly goggled and with the straps of a leather aviator's cap flapping about his grizzled ears, Rolph sat hunched over the handlebars. Suddenly something in the sidecar stirred. Then a small hand reached out and tugged frantically at Rolph's leg.

Rolph turned, gasped and hit the brakes. The Whizzer skidded to a rubber-burning halt.

'Holy Snouts! Is that you, Arthur Snout?' gasped old Rolph, staggering to his feet, goggles akimbo.

'Yes, sir,' the stunned Hound replied.

'What in the Cat-blazes do you think you're doing in my sidecar?'

'Sleeping, sir.'

Lonely could not explain to his headmaster that the dark old woodshed at the back of the garden had become his refuge, the one place he felt safe from Marvin. More and more often, when Marvin and his hench Hounds were on the prowl, he would slip out through the squeaky fly-screen door and creep down the gravel path, under the lacy-leafed Brumbella tree to the sanctuary of the shed. No one knew of this haven, not even Kelzie.

'Sleeping?' spluttered Rolph. 'You have a bed back at the Orphanage for that.'

'I'm very sorry, sir. I was hiding… I just fell asleep and—'

'Yes, yes!' interrupted Rolph. 'No harm's been done.'

'If it's all right with you, sir, I'll just be heading back to the Orphanage now…'

Lonely was about to clamber out of the sidecar when Rolph stopped him.

He could hardly allow the lad to go back to the Orphanage since that could mean waking Bella, which would mean trouble! There could be 'enquiries'.

What to do? What to do?

Lonely sat anxiously in the sidecar awaiting his fate.

Assuming his most headmasterly tone, Rolph addressed him.

'Now listen here, young Snout, what you have done, by sneaking into my sidecar, is absolutely unconscionable. I have a good mind to take you by the ear and march you directly back to the Orphanage.' His voice softened somewhat. 'However, given your obvious interest in all things musical, I am prepared to overlook your little indiscretion and turn this unfortunate incident into an

educational excursion.'

Lonely stared
at him blankly.

Then Rolph leaned
over him with a
conspiratorial wink.

'Tonight,
young Arthur
Snout, you are to
come with me

Houndster Whizzer

to Revellers Green. But you must not breathe a word of this to anyone, ever!' He cast a nervous glance back towards the Orphanage. 'Especially Mrs Bostock.'

A bewildered Lonely nodded vehemently.

Rolph powered the noisy machine off down the road, so fast that the little Hound's whiskers tingled and his eyes watered. The streetlights of Tumbleton Avenue were as nothing compared to the glow of Lonely's snout. 'Revellers Green!' he whispered to himself. The name itself was almost a mythical incantation. Like the other Houndlings, Lonely had been given stern warnings concerning 'the Green'. 'It is absolutely no place for a young Houndling! No good will come of a visit there.' They'd all heard the rumours of whisky and wild music; now as the Houndster rounded the corner and sped towards the docks, Lonely glimpsed the forbidden place.

CHAPTER V

Dwarf-Hounds, Blues and Green

I owe all my blues to the Green.

—Lonely Dog interview in *Howling Moon*

*M*usic historians agree that Lonely Dog changed the music of Alveridgea for ever. But the same writers argue bitterly about what, and who, helped mould his unique style. Most date these seminal influences to the years that followed his time at the Orphanage. They are wrong.

The definitive, life-changing event that was to shape Arthur Snout occurred on the night he crept into a cane sidecar and was whisked away by Rolph Flannegan to Revellers Green.

This was a place Lonely had read of only in faded newspapers, heard of only in the lyrics of crackling recordings in the Orphanage attic: snatched sepia images, scratched sounds. Now, here it was, full and throbbing.

Beneath the massive Tumbleroot trees that lined the meandering paths of Revellers Green was a veritable gypsy camp of canvas awnings, vaudeville hoardings and carnival-style hawkers' tents. Old tramp Hounds lay under newspaper bedspreads oblivious to the passing crowds.

In the treetops above were the straggly nests of tree Hounds, nimble buskers who preferred their elevated platforms of driftwood and bric-a-brac to normal paw-on-the-ground Hound abodes. They descended on ropes to entertain the crowds and re-ascended, caps full of coins.

Lonely clambered out of the sidecar, awestruck, his eyes as big as the wheels on Rolph's bike, simply enchanted. He struggled to keep pace with old Rolph, who was determinedly weaving his way through the crowd looking for his fellow skifflers. A jester Hound suddenly hove into view, precariously perched atop enormous stilts, all crazy hat and long striped trousers, calmly juggling a clutch of greasy pigs as if it was the most normal thing in all the world. He winked at the little Hound then strode away into the crowd.

Lonely stopped to watch a brassy-haired, tattooed Houndette, sagging beneath a lifetime of make-up. To his astonishment, she swallowed a ball of fire and then, with a dramatic belch, blew a magnificent flame that flambéed a fistful of fish kebabs! She gave him one for free, beaming a crack-toothed smile.

Suddenly a roar erupted from one corner of the Green, spinning the Houndling's head round just in time to see a Hound in a shabby clown-suit shoot out of a cannon and soar over the bay. Amazing!

Everywhere Arthur turned there was something more to overwhelm his senses: the smells of exotic food, the rhythmic beat of the bongo, the swirling colours of flamboyant tree-Hound dancers, not to mention a small troupe of costumed Shakespearean Hounds in full recital. And rising above the joyous cacophony was a strange sound, distinctively different from anything Lonely had ever heard before.

He pushed through the swell of Hounds surrounding him, following the high-pitched noise to the centre of the Green, trying in vain to keep sight of Rolph, who ploughed ahead as if embarrassed by the small Hound he had in tow. Gathered there, around a rather torpid fountain, was the oddest sight of the evening thus far. Lonely had in fact smelled them before he had laid eyes on them. Cats!

A quartet of Cats to be exact, each wearing a freshly pressed tuxedo and crisp bow tie – attire that deeply impressed the sartorially minded little Hound. He had never encountered a live Cat before. Their smell was sweeter than that of a Hound but Arthur did not find it as threatening as his headmaster and the Baron had led him to expect.

The quartet were just completing a startling composition for violin

Revellers Green

and cello and Lonely wondered at the dazzling dexterity with which they played these strange instruments. When the piece ended, Lonely clapped spontaneously, only to realize suddenly that he was their only audience member. The rest of the Houndish crowd stalked past the group, snouts disdainfully averted. Some even spat in disgust.

The elegant leader of the quartet, a Tom Cat with trimmed tail and waxed whiskers, bowed low and extended a white-gloved hand to the startled Lonely.

'Thank you, kind sir!' he said in a clipped but friendly tone. 'So nice to meet a Hound who appreciates the Classics!' Then, observing the small Hound's attire, added appreciatively, 'And one who obviously takes pride in his appearance! My name is Travis, Travis Furlington, and these are my esteemed accomplices, Limerick, Gregorion and Chadwick.'

Shaking their hands, Lonely immediately noticed how smooth and soft they felt, so unlike a calloused Hound's.

Travis smiled knowingly. 'Have you never seen a Cat before, my good friend?'

'No, never,' replied Lonely.

'Well, I must admit that until recently we had never seen a Hound either.'

'That was until we arrived in Port Alveridge and began giving recitals here on the Green,' Limerick piped up, leaning closer to Lonely and adding, with a wrinkled nose, 'It took us a day or two to adjust to the Hound smell – it's quite distinctive you know!'

'It would seem, however, that our style of music is as foreign to Hound ears as theirs is to ours.'

Lonely was about to say that he had enjoyed their music, but Travis continued, 'This is only a temporary engagement though. We are awaiting the reopening of the famous Catside Academy of Music, where we have all been accepted as students. Chadwick and I have both been offered solo parts in the forthcoming production of Leonisky's *La Vengeance de la Marionnettiste*.'

Lonely stared blankly.

'*Revenge of the Puppeteer!*' laughed Travis. 'You must come to Catside and see us perform. I'll arrange for tickets to be sent to your parents.'

Lonely didn't have the heart to tell Travis that he was an orphan and that even if tickets were sent to the Orphanage, he would never be allowed to venture into Catside to attend. Sensing something was amiss, Travis quickly tapped his bow on his violin.

'Gentlemen! Let us play our little friend a tune sure to lift his spirits…

'Frivolous's *Anthem to Spring!*'

The quartet of Cats sprang to life and Lonely stood, captivated once again by the strangely beautiful music they played…

'Arthur! ARTHUR!'

Rolph's voice snapped Lonely out of his reverie.

'I've been looking for you everywhere!'

The old Headmaster grabbed his hand and tugged him through the crowd, casting a disdainful scowl at the Cat quartet.

'Come on, boy. That puss-screeching is not fit music for a Hound's ears. Your education of true Houndish music will begin with a taste of authentic live Houndskiffle and Tap.'

He led Lonely to the outer edge of the Green, away from the ferment and froth of the crowd. Here, the garish lights from the carnival cast long shadows, fingers of light illuminating a group of old Hounds gathered around a crackling oil-drum brazier. A dozen or so pairs of rheumy eyes and grizzled snouts turned as he and Rolph stepped into the glow.

'You got yourself a guitar-caddy, Flannegan?' asked one old Hound with a twinkle in his voice.

Rolph directed Lonely to a spot by the fire, alongside a gnarly Tumbleroot. 'This is one of my boys, young Arthur Snout. He promises to sit still and listen quietly.'

'Come to hear some real Houndskiffle, eh?' chuckled a toothless Hound, a washboard between his knees.

Lonely could not find his voice to answer, but his eyes were big as

After Midnight

banjos. In the distance the cannon roared, sending another clown skyward, but the Houndling barely noticed. He was transfixed by the old Hounds, seated on camp chairs and stools around the fire, wearing grubby overalls and knotted bandanas…

…and by their marvellous instruments.

Battered guitars, dented saxophones, a trumpet made from an old car horn, even a rickety piano on bicycle wheels fitted with a pram handle.

Rolph opened his worn guitar case, took out his five-string Alveridgean. As he began to strum, the rich, vibrant notes filled Lonely's ears, then his mind and finally his soul.

For the first time in his life, Lonely saw his headmaster smile.

Lonely's little tail wagged like a metronome. He had a front-row seat at a real Houndskiffle performance!

Houndskiffle and Tap was the pre-eminent sound of Houndside, its distinctive thump and twang emanating from kitchens, clubs and street corners. Its rough charms perfectly suited the easy-going Hound lifestyle. Big on beat and totally without pretension, it was music that could be played by anyone with a pair of spoons or a boombox bass.

Lonely had often lain awake in his Orphanage bed and listened to the Houndskiffle that seeped under the doors from Bella's twin-valve radio; sometimes he caught snatches of Rolph's furtive playing as he passed the Headmaster's study late at night, the old Hound's slippered feet tapping the floorboards in time with his strumming. *Boom chicka, boom chicka, strum chicka, strum…*

The other musicians, following Rolph's lead, began to join the jam. Arthur Snout closed his eyes and lay back in the warm, sweet-smelling grass, his mind drifting with the spiralling embers as they soared heaven-ward, carried on the hypnotic thump and twang.

> Oh the sea is so cruel, and the wind cuts like a knife
>
> And sweethearts and lovers they only cause strife
>
> For only one thing is true and won't surely part
>
> A five-string guitar and one broken heart

In the hush that followed the end of the song, as performer and audience were still caught up in its last echoes, Lonely suddenly got to his feet and stepped into the ring, his little face burning with passion. To everyone's astonishment, he said softly but determinedly: 'One day I will play and the whole world will hear!'

He sat down quietly and the old Hounds simply raised their aged heads, casting knowing winks in Rolph's embarrassed direction. Then with a 'One... two... three...' they picked up their instruments and skiffled on into the night.

By the time Rolph and Arthur had said goodbye to their fellow Revellers and shuffled back to the Houndster it was almost dawn, the crowd and clamour melting away with the darkness. Only a few tree Hounds remained, shimmying up their ropes to their nests; a yawning fire-eater slouched home. As a warm breeze blew across the Green, an empty Wilks bottle rolled eerily along the path beneath the stark Tumbleroots.

Rolph reverently loaded his guitar case and then Arthur into the sidecar and swung his leg over the old bike's tank. He kick-started the

Whizzer, which belched into life, and in a cloud of choking smoke they rumbled back towards Tumbleton Avenue. Lost in his thoughts, Rolph did not notice Travis and the Cat quartet waving from the roadside, but Lonely caught sight of them, still immaculately attired.

'Good luck, little friend! Come see us in Catside...' Travis cried, but his voice was lost in the roar of the bike's four-stroke.

The Headmaster said not a word on the ride back to the Orphanage, but now and then he looked down at the little Hound in the sidecar and thought of Lonely's promise: 'I will play... and the whole world will hear!'

'What to do?' Rolph shook his head and muttered to himself. 'What to do?'

Back at the Orphanage, Lonely tiptoed into the dormitory – though this was hardly necessary since the Hounds were snoring so loudly. He climbed into bed, but found he could not sleep, his mind still buzzing with the wonders of Revellers Green, the music, and the haunting refrain from Rolph's song:

> For only one thing is true and won't surely part
> A five-string guitar and one broken heart

The little Hound's dream that night would stay with him for a long time. He stood in a shaft of Blue Moon light, a shimmering guitar in his hands, staring out across a sea of faces that seemed to stretch as far as the horizon. And then he sang.

attered Memories and Faded Flags

Let all Houndkind rejoice and sing
Beneath the moon's blue light
For joyous madness fills the air
This midsummer of delight!

— King Alver II, Great Hound of all Alveridgea

'*S*o there I was, with cannonballs raining down around
me,' boomed the Baron of Beaconsfield, though in his
slurred voice 'cannonballs' sounded more like 'cannibals'.

There was a titter from the class and Headmaster Flannegan rapped his
cane on his desk, sending a cloud of white chalk dust wafting upwards.
The Houndlings, crowded behind hard wooden desks, were, as usual,
inattentive and bored. Rolph Flannegan often tried to enliven his lessons
on Houndish history by inviting speakers to address the students. His old
friend the Baron was a frequent guest, and right now was holding forth
on his favourite subject – a crucial episode in Hound history – the Battle
of Beaconsfield.

'The Cats held the high ground behind a battery of cannons,' he went
on, oblivious to the fact that only Arthur Snout was listening. 'I was
ordered to take my regiment and charge Beacons Hill.' The Baron began
rearranging pencils and chalk on the Headmaster's desk to form battalions ready for attack. 'I formed my brave Hounds into a flying wedge.

Then, with bugle call and flags flying, I drew my sabre and we charged.'

Lonely was enthralled as much by the rhythm of the Baron's words as by his story. His head was still filled with the music of the previous night's excursion to the Green, where he'd glimpsed a new and different side to his old Headmaster; where he had seen and heard an aspect of Houndside that he had never known before.

There was a crash as the Baron sent pencils, chalk and books crashing to the ground.

The Baron

'Half my brave Hounds were mown down by cannon fire!' The Baron's gluey eyes blazed like musket fire, as if the whole scene were being played out before him.

'By the time we reached the summit, I had barely half my Hounds remaining. "Show the bloody Moggies your steel, lads!" I cried. "Slash and Thrust!" Dead Cats piled up around us. By noon they had faltered and by the moon's rising we had our sabres to their throats! The Battle of Beaconsfield was won.'

While his classmates went on fooling around, Lonely stared at the Baron, who by now had climbed atop the Headmaster's chair and, for a moment, looked like the Hound he had been in his youth: fearless, clear of eye, noble of snout. Lonely could picture him standing on Beacons Hill, tattered flags flapping, the blood of a thousand Moggies dripping from his sword.

Then, just as suddenly, the Baron was back to his aged present, slowly clambering down from his summit, his face haunted by the spectre of a past so ghastly that he seemed to slump into the chair.

'Alas,' his voice was almost inaudible now, 'it was a false freedom. Not long after, even as we celebrated victory, a messenger approached with a communiqué from the mad Hound King himself, King Alver II, Great Hound of all Alveridgea, in which he proclaimed that he had just signed "Terms of Surrender" with the Moggies. *Terms of bloody surrender!*'

Old Rolph laid a calming hand on the Baron's shoulder; this was no language to use before young, impressionable Hounds.

'Terms of surrender? We had them by the throats, we had won the Battle of Beaconsfield.'

Alas, it was true, something that most Hounds would never speak of. Whilst they had won the battle, they had lost the war. They felt their king had sold them out all those years back. The very same day, while brave Hounds celebrated victory at Beaconsfield, not five hundred miles south, in Tolle, Feline nobles came bearing gifts to the King's court. King Alver II, an aged and exceedingly droopy bloodhound, spent his days slumped in his throne, staring cross-eyed at his toys scattered around him. The Moggies bought his signature and seal for an armful of Houndling toys. One toy train was the price for all of Greater Alveridgea. He signed the treaty while a thousand knights stood by in his court and did nothing.

Even the rowdiest of the Houndlings had fallen silent now as tears trickled down the Baron's grizzled snout and his creaking body shook with sobs. At Rolph's insistence the class gave the speaker three cheers. As the Headmaster showed the Baron out, Lonely thought he glimpsed a tear in old Rolph's eyes too. Lonely had always been fond of his headmaster, but witnessing him the previous night as a Houndskiffler, a Reveller; watching his arthritic fingers dance along the fretboard of his guitar, listening to him sing; and now seeing him caught up in the passion and fury of their history, Lonely's respect for him was fast turning into hero worship.

When Lonely had tried, in a fumbling way, to thank Rolph for taking him to the Green, the old Hound had simply silenced him with a stern finger to the lips. 'We will talk no more of this.'

From her desk next to his, Kelzie was looking at him strangely.

She leaned over and whispered, 'Where were you last night?'

He turned to her, his brown eyes wide with surprise.

'What…? When?' he said too quickly.

'I couldn't sleep. I saw you and Headmaster Flannegan coming back late. Where were you?' Her eyes sparkled as if hoping to be let in on some thrilling and forbidden secret.

Lonely liked Kelzie. Over the years, they had become close; apart from Bronson, she was his one true friend. In late-night conversations in the music room, he and Kelzie had often shared their secrets and dreams with one

Kelzie

another. He sometimes thought of her as the nearest he had to a sister, though of late his feelings for the little Houndette with the pigtails and limpid eyes had begun to grow into something he could not put into words, but which he dimly realized was beyond a brotherly affection.

Kelzie was the quiet one. She too was a little apart from the other Houndettes in the Orphanage. Even though their dormitories were in separate wings, whenever they met, she didn't feel shy around him. She didn't think he was unusual, and didn't giggle like the other Houndettes when he walked by. In fact, Kelzie saw Lonely as more sensitive and grown up than all the others, as someone she could talk to about anything.

Lonely had a dilemma. What should he tell her about his excursion with old Rolph? He had been sworn to secrecy. Still, she stared into his troubled eyes, waiting for an answer, and Lonely was only saved from breaking his oath by the sudden whack of the Headmaster's cane on his desk.

'Pay attention! Or I shall have to administer a "sharp reminder" to anybody not listening!'

The class knew all about the Headmaster's 'sharp reminders' and many still bore such aides-memoire as welts on their backsides.

'Following the Battle of Beaconsfield, we shall turn to…'

Muted groans from the class.

'…the bloody Wars of Blackenrowe.'

Sudden interest from the class.

'The Felinean cats had sailed their armada of warships across the Snoring Strait beneath the blood-red banner of their brutal leader, Felinicus the Merciless…' The old Headmaster began solemnly but soon warmed to his task, holding the Houndlings quite spellbound.

'As they engaged in battle on the northern shores of Alveridgea, Feline hordes were also secretly landing on the beaches of Blackenrowe. The Black-Hounds, as the residents of Blackenrowe were known, had joined with their old allies to defend Alveridgea, leaving Blackenrowe vulnerable and unguarded. Sending Feline troops to engage the allies on Alveridgean soil was a decoy; the prize was Blackenrowe.

'The Felineans began ravaging everything in their path, moving north, burning Hound villages and hamlets before them. But they were not ready for what lay waiting. Flying low and stealthy over the cold waste-lands of Terriean came the Terriers, thousands of them. Fast-talking, small in stature, but fearless aviators, they came in single-cylinder aircraft

The Terriers

built from stilt-skin, wood and glue. They mowed down the Felineans with endless fire from wing-mounted scatterguns. There was great loss on both sides as Felinean gunners eventually sounded the retreat.'

The lunch bell trilled. The spell was broken. A horde of hungry young Hounds bolted for the door. Only Lonely remained sitting at his desk. Kelzie calling to him from the doorway, but he did not hear her.

Rolph looked up. 'Best get a move on, young Arthur, or you'll be late for lunch.'

But Lonely was far away in a place where history and music mingled, where the clash of swords and the strum of strings were bathed in the light of a huge Blue Moon; he was back in his dream, staring out at the sea of faces, clutching his guitar.

'Arthur?' barked Rolph.

'Lonely?' called Kelzie urgently.

'Lonely! Lonely!' cried the vast audience in his dream.

It was pandemonium in the dining hall. A long line of famished Hounds eagerly waited for the serving hatch to open, beating tin plates and spoons in expectation as the aroma of freshly baked bread and ham-bone soup wafted from Bella's kitchen. Lonely was the final Hound to trail in, joining Kelzie at the back of the rowdy queue.

There was a time when Bronson would have been at the head of the group. His steely-eyed presence at the hatch was usually enough to keep even the most recalcitrant Houndling in line – and if that failed, a swift boot in the hind-quarters would do the trick.

But Bronson had left the Orphanage in disgrace.

Nasty rumours had begun to circulate about his night-time escapades at the Port's pool halls.

It was true that he often sneaked out after dark for some fun with his biker buddies, but the rumours put about by Marvin had accused him of gambling and drinking, of brawling and bad company – anything, in fact, young Marvin could think of that was contrary to Orphanage rules.

In his own stoic way, Bronson had tried to refute the tittle-tattle but, as the old Hound saying goes, 'Gossip spreads like Cat turd on a shagpile rug'. And, with Marvin's malicious help, it had soiled the entire carpet.

When the Orphanage Board of Governors had demanded that Bronson be expelled, Rolph fought the ruling tooth and nail. But before the sentence fell, Bronson had made his own decision: he packed up and left in the middle of the night. No one knew where he had gone.

All the Houndlings missed Bronson, but Lonely felt the loss of his big brother, his protector, most of all. Only Marvin had reason to smile about his absence.

With Bronson gone, Marvin and his thuggish mates had free rein to stalk the classrooms for their prey and any Houndling who stood in their way could find him- or herself cruelly beaten and locked in the freezing coal-cellar. Lonely was accustomed to it; he had spent a few chilly nights there already, ears and snout throbbing from the cold and the bruises, his usually pristine clothes ripped and smeared in coal-dust. He had learned to endure the beatings, learned to shut out the pain, even learned to hold back his tears, but he had never learned to stand up to Marvin's bullying.

Until the night that Lonely heard Kelzie's muffled howls coming from the girls' dormitory.

He had dashed down the midnight hallway to find Marvin and his thugs off-limits, dragging Kelzie by her pigtail ears towards the coal-cellar.

'Let her go!' Lonely growled, his face a mask of anger.

Marvin turned, holding Kelzie tightly in front of him.

'What did you say, pussy-pants?'

Lonely felt his hands ball into fists.

'You heard me. Let her go!'

'Or what?' snarled Marvin, revealing a row of sharp canines and savagely tugging Kelzie's ears so hard she cried out.

Lonely exploded. Head down, he charged at Marvin like an enraged bull, catching him off-balance and sending him crashing into the wall with such force it splintered beneath him. Then, his fists a blur, Lonely began to pummel and pound the cowardly Hound as Marvin's astonished thugs fled. It was Kelzie who finally managed to pull him away.

Marvin struggled to his feet, his snout dripping blood, his eyes malevolent pin-pricks.

Suddenly Bella's voice rang out from downstairs. 'What the blazes is going on up there?'

'You are dead meat!' hissed Marvin. 'DEAD MEAT!'

Lonely stared him down, panting so hard he could hardly speak.

'NEVER…' he gasped, 'Never touch her again!'

Since that incident, Marvin had been wary of Lonely, watching him from a distance with baleful eyes. Although Lonely knew that Marvin was just biding his time, for the first time in his life he felt emboldened. He had stood up to Marvin. Maybe it was his former protector Bronson's influence, maybe it had something to do with his feelings for Kelzie, but in the days that followed his magical night on Revellers Green, Lonely put his new-found confidence down to the music that had been echoing inside him ever since.

Around midnight every night, Lonely took to creeping out of the dormitory and quietly down the stairs to the dark music room. There, with the Trumaine seven-and-a-half-string on his lap, he poured out all his hopes, his frustrations and his dreams in song. Over many nights, he taught himself many songs – he had even tried to make up one or two more – but his favourite, the one that stirred him, was the old Van Trong song he had learned by heart from the records in the attic:

> Boss Man you can beat me, you can even dock my pay
>
> But Boss Man you get ready 'cause here comes Judgement Day
>
> It just ain't right
>
> It just ain't right
>
> I'm gonna stand up and fight
>
> 'Cause it just ain't right!

CHAPTER VII

Silk Suits and Kelp Cigars

Thirty silver pieces
That's the going price for betrayal
Thirty dirty pieces
Each one a coffin nail

—Hank Rootenfurg,
'Hand Me Down My Hanging Rope'

A.K. Ruddegan lit a cigar and watched the smoke curl like a rat's tail towards the ceiling. His glass-sided office was illuminated by a simple desk lamp that cast sinister shadows on his face. Outside, night curled around the Cannery like a Hound looking for scraps; the moon rose over the four chimneys like a hanged man. The Mayor took a long pull on his cigar.

'I'd offer you one, but you don't smoke cigars, do you?' he purred.

'I'll stick to my pipe,' a hoarse voice mumbled from the shadowy corner.

A match flared and faded, to be replaced by the dull glow of a baccy-bowl and the acrid smell of pipe smoke.

Ruddegan leaned back in his leather chair, stroking his silver whiskers with his free hand.

'How long have we been meeting like this, my friend?' he enquired silkily.

'Thirteen years come next Blue Moon,' the figure in the shadows replied, sucking on his pipe for a moment. 'But you're no friend of mine.'

'Thirteen years! And still you consider me an enemy!' Ruddegan feigned shock. 'Come, come, at least you might consider me a business partner.'

'Consider me in a hurry!' came the tart reply. 'If you've got the money I'll take it and leave. The smell of Cat burns my nostrils.'

'Such hostility!'

Ruddegan laughed, a sneering little staccato. He reached into his desk drawer, took out a fat envelope, held it to his nose, and sniffed.

'800 Alvers. Be careful, it smells of Cat!'

'800 Alvers? We agreed 1500.'

Ruddegan lifted his hands in the air, trailing cigar smoke.

'We agreed nothing, *my friend*,' he replied, his voice almost a whisper. 'In fact, I have been reconsidering our business partnership and I'm minded to terminate it.'

'What? Why?' The hoarse voice was now tinged with fear. 'I bring you what you want, don't I?'

'Trifles!' Ruddegan snorted derisively. 'You bring me trifles such as anyone might bring. You know what I really want, and so far you have utterly failed to deliver. But I am a reasonable Feline, I shall give you until next week…'

'Or what?'

'Or I shall be forced to leak certain stories to the press.'

Ruddegan languidly brushed ash from the lapel of his silk suit.

'Unsavoury stories that would put paid to your career and probably drive you out of Port Alveridge in shame!'

He got to his feet, his eyes like glowing coals.

'And where would your poor little orphan Houndlings be then, Headmaster?'

Rolph Flannegan stepped out of the shadows, gaunt, defeated. Without looking A. K. Ruddegan in the eye, he scooped up the Manila envelope and shambled out of the Cannery office and into the night.

CHAPTER VIII

Indigo Madness

My Grandaddy told me
He said 'son yer listen here,
Ain't no one gonna stand when the
South wind runs her fingers thru yer hair!'
The East wind comes all sultry
Like a woman in the night
And the West wind's
Like a sailor, staggering drunken in the light.
That old North wind whispers promises that she just can't keep.
But that cruel South wind is the bitch you'll never ever beat.

— Whisky Lips Willy, from the bootleg tapes recorded in
The Rusty Razor Nightclub with Sly Syd Groover

*T*he wind had changed direction. The summer
skies seemed more vibrant, more spectacular than
anyone could remember. Normally nonchalant Hounds
stopped each other in the streets of Port Alveridge to
comment on this unusual change in the cosmos.

'It's comin'.' Old Hounds began to turn their snouts to the balmy
breeze. 'I can smell it on the wind!'

Down at Revellers Green the entire carnival crowd paused to turn
their snouts heavenward.

'What's comin'?' asked younger Hounds. 'What's on the wind?'

'Madness!' chuckled the old ones. 'Midsummer Madness!'

The glorious summer sky exploded in one final phantasmagoric dis-
play, then dissolved into night. Every Hound in all of Greater Alveridgea
turned to watch as twilight gave way to inky black. Over the horizon,
flaring like a beacon, came what each one of them dreamed of: an indigo
Blue Moon.

At the Orphanage, Rolph, Bella and a crowd of Houndlings stood on the porch watching it rise.

'It's Midsummer Madness!' the Headmaster shouted with glee, then turned to Bella and did something the Houndlings had never seen him do before – he kissed her full on the lips!

'Pack the bus, pack food, pack guitars—'

'Pack the Houndlings?' asked Bella, still stunned from his kiss.

'It's the Blue Moon!' he laughed as he whooped and danced up the stairs. 'Pack everything! We're going to Marmalade Mountain!'

For as long as Lonely could remember he had heard tales of Midsummer Madness, the festival that took place only once in a Blue Moon – an astrological phenomenon that occurred unannounced, about once every decade, give or take a few years. When the Blue Moon rose, factories closed – even the mighty Cannery – and roads became crammed with rumbling Houndsters, chugging buses, squeaking bicycles, honking Trunkriders. A hundred-mile traffic jam of tooting horns all heading for Marmalade Mountain, where a wonderful natural amphitheatre overlooking a sparkling bay provided the perfect venue for Midsummer Madness.

The stage was a massive granite bluff shaped like a giant Hound's paw. In the shadow of the mountain a sea of tents, marquees and lean-tos would suddenly appear. As day gave way to night, the stage would blaze with lights as ten thousand Hounds waited expectantly. And then – music! Ballads, blues, anthems, folk and of course… Houndskiffle!

Midsummer Madness was a jamboree of Hound music, Hound dance and Hound pride – from the raw and raucous sounds of the mountain

Juke Hounds to the mellower vibe of Port Alveridge blues.

Already, pandemonium was spreading through Greater Alveridgea. Mother Hounds emptied whole pantries into bulging hampers, Father Hounds stuffed moth-eaten tents into the boots of old cars. And everywhere, Houndlings weaved between their feet, wide-eyed and dizzy with anticipation.

From the dormitory window Lonely stared entranced as the Blue Moon cast a silvery path across the Esparrow Sea, a path that would lead them all the way up the coast to Marmalade Mountain. Downstairs, Rolph flung open the garage doors. The decrepit Orphanage bus greeted him with a bleary smile of bent bumpers and grimy headlights.

'Get the Houndlings organized while I try and get this old girl ready!' he called to Bella, who had four yapping Houndlings by the scruff of their tiny necks and was herding a dozen more inside.

She was already in an advanced stage of dither as she ran round her kitchen snatching loaves of bread, grabbing jars of jam and generally trying to gather as much food as would be required for… for who knew how long!

No one could predict how many days a Midsummer Madness Festival might last. 'It'll run as long as it's needed and finish when it's time,' old Hounds would tell you sagely, tapping their baccy-pipes against their snouts.

Soon Lonely was running excitedly down the garden path towards the woodshed. Rolph had instructed him to fetch his old guitar.

'I left it in the sidecar,' he said with a knowing wink, as he stuck his head under the bonnet of the dilapidated bus, extracting a recalcitrant spark plug like a dentist with a bad tooth. 'You run there now, little Snout, and bring me my five-string.'

In his excited haste to fetch the Headmaster's guitar, Lonely failed to notice that he was being followed by a shadowy figure.

Marvin.

He had spotted Rolph talking to Lonely and had seen the little Hound race off eagerly down the garden path.

'What's he up to?' Marvin wondered as he slunk along the rascalberry bushes that lined the pathway. 'He's heading for the woodshed. But that's always locked…'

The Woodshed

He watched in astonishment as little Lonely scrambled under the loosened plank at the rear of the shed. His eyes narrowed and his smile betrayed his grandmother's liaison with a sailor-wolf long ago.

'So that's where you've been hiding all this time!'

He was just about to sneak up to the grimy window and see what Lonely was doing when a shrill voice echoed down the pathway. It was Bella and she sounded flustered.

'Marvin Bostock? Is that you lurking down there by the woodshed? Well you get your furry little butt back up here this instant. There's work to do! Mr Flannegan's got the bus ready now and we all need to be getting on. And where in St Bernard's name is wee Arthur Snout? Is he down there with you?'

Marvin was about to reluctantly reply that, yes, Arthur Snout was indeed to be found at the bottom of the garden, but he paused as a deliciously wicked idea bubbled up in his fermented mind.

'No! Mr Flannegan asked me to come look for him myself, but he sure isn't down here! Must've got on the bus by himself.'

Bella had no time to answer. Rolph was already revving the old bus engine and calling for her to load up, and Houndlings of all shapes and sizes were yelling for assistance.

Marvin waited till she had gone, then tiptoed to the woodshed window and peered inside. He could see Lonely struggling with a large tarpaulin, then watched in astonishment as the little Hound finally removed it to reveal the Houndster Whizzer!

Unaware that his every move was being watched, Lonely gently lifted Rolph's treasured guitar out of the sidecar. It was much heavier than he had imagined and he strained to drag it across the woodshed floor. Out-side, he could hear the incessant toot of the horn and knew that unless he was quick he might miss the bus. He reached the door, heaving the cumbersome instrument in his wake, but realized to his horror that it was locked from the outside. Rolph hadn't thought to give him the key and he hadn't thought to ask.

Hurriedly now, with the horn bleating and Bella's voice booming, Lonely dragged the guitar towards the rear of the shed and frantically tried to push it under the loose-plank exit. It jammed stuck! He strained again, his little back bent with exertion, his snout wrinkling with deter-mination. Suddenly the guitar case shot through the gap with such abruptness that Lonely crashed into the woodshed wall with a resound-ing thwack. He heard a voice on the other side, a voice he had learned to be very wary of.

'Hey, little Hound, let me help you with that guitar.'

'Marvin? Is that you?' asked Lonely as he began to crawl under the loosened plank.

'Yeah! Old Flanagan asked me to come help get his precious guitar.'

Lonely breathed a sigh of relief. 'Thanks! For a moment I was wor-ried that I wasn't going to be able to get out with…'

Marvin sneered. 'I said I'd come to get old Flannegan's guitar – not you!'

Lonely began to scramble out of the shed, fearing that Marvin was up to his old tricks. But the once-loose plank was now unmovable! He heard the sound of falling timber, the thud of logs against the wooden wall of the shed. In a blinding moment he realized what Marvin was up to. He had overturned the pile of Cracklewood and blocked the only exit out of the woodshed. Marvin's cruel laughter confirmed his worst fears.

'Hey, Lonely Dog! Better get cracking or you'll miss the bus! Wouldn't want to miss the festival, now would we?'

Lonely began to beat frantically on the woodshed walls, his little fists a flurry of desperation.

'Marvin! Marvin! Please let me out!'

Marvin's laughter grew fainter and fainter. He wasn't coming back.

'Bella! Mr Flannegan!' he shouted despairingly, hoisting himself up onto the seat of the Whizzer to look out of the grubby window.

He could see the bus, loaded with Houndlings, ready to rumble off down the driveway.

'Wait! Don't go!' he wailed in vain. He watched with a sickening feeling as the bus slowly disappeared down the driveway, the leering faces of Marvin and his latest crony Jasper at the back window.

Lonely slumped on to the seat and sobbed.

Why? Why had they left him behind? Hadn't Rolph done a headcount? Surely Bella would have noticed that he was missing?

In fact Bella had not noticed. Marvin had anticipated this eventuality and had rifled Lonely's bag for one of his neatly pressed suits. This he had stuffed with a pillow and with the aid of an old football had, with Jasper's help, settled the dummy between them in the far corner of the bus.

When Bella did the final headcount, with Rolph impatiently revving the accelerator, and Houndlings all fighting for space, she had taken Marvin's word that 'Lonely's in the back with us.' Now they were gone and all that was left behind was an eerie silence hanging like a cloud of bus exhaust beneath the Blue Moon.

Tears pooled in the sad corners of his eyes and flowed down his snout. Frantically he searched for another rotten weatherboard that he could push through. Board after board he tried, until with a great heave he finally broke through and sprinted off down Tumbleton Avenue, desperately hoping to catch up.

But the bus, like his dreams of going to the Midsummer Madness Festival, had disappeared into the night. He had missed his golden opportunity. That fateful evening his shoulders slumped – some say he never unslumped them.

He returned to the empty dining hall to find the Orphanage as quiet as the grave. He sat for hours by the big bay window in the dining room overlooking Tumbleton Avenue, hoping against hope that the old Orphanage bus would pull into the drive and that he'd hear Bella say, 'We came back for you, little Arthur Snout!' By midnight it was obvious that nobody was coming back for him. Lonely put his head in his hands and wept.

'Why did they leave me?' he sobbed.

To his astonishment a little voice answered.

'Not just you, Lonely. They've left me as well.'

He looked up. Standing in the dining room doorway, caught in the blue glow of the moon, was a small Houndette holding her flannel blanket. It was Kelzie, petite and shy, with her slim snout and moist button nose. Little did he know that from that dark night he would gain something special – a deeper friendship. Her deep brown eyes were red rimmed from

Houndlings' Reward

crying and Arthur noticed that she shivered as she sobbed in the cold night air. Ever the gentleman, he took off his jacket and draped it over Kelzie's slender shoulders.

'How did you get left behind?' he asked her gently. 'I thought I was the only one.'

'I think I was asleep,' she whimpered, barely holding back the tears. 'I guess they just forgot about me.'

Lonely looked at her sweet face and thought how hard it would be for anyone to forget it.

'Bella would never forget you… or me!' he said with a new-found passion. 'This is all Marvin's doing.'

He told her about the woodshed and Rolph's bike, and how he'd chased the bus. They stood silent for a long while, two little Hounds silhouetted in the big bay window, staring out at the Blue Moon rising high over the Esparrow Sea.

Shyly he turned to Kelzie, took her small hand in his and said, 'One day you and I will go to the festival and nothing, and no one, will stop us! In the meantime, let me sing you a song.'

CHAPTER IX

Mask in the Squeaky Wheelbarrow

Grab your cane, polish your hat,
Don't forget your cufflinks and a crimson cravat!
Dust off your tails, shine your spats
We're stepping out in Catside
Rat-A-Tat-Cat!

—From 'Nine Lives and Counting!'
by Baz Burlington and his Big Band

*T*he Alveridge Home for Cats sat high and haughty
on the sunny slopes of North Tolleston in Catside. Though
it too was an orphanage, it was a world away from its
poorer Houndside cousin: manicured lawns like velvet
carpet rolled up to the imposing entrance steps, brass
fixtures gleamed and the windows glinted. Here, within
the calm, cream-coloured walls, orphaned Kitterlings were
tutored in the Feline arts of sophistication and grooming.

The head matron was known simply as Nan, although her full name,
embossed in gold leaf on her office door, was Madame Nancy Van Frill-
ing. Nan ran the Home for Cats with the precision of a fine gold watch,
but the Kitterlings in her care adored her and Nan loved them in return.

Not that she would let any infraction of the rules go unpunished.
There was no Hound-like tomfoolery in her well-run establishment. She
demanded, and received, perfect behaviour and impeccable manners.

One night, as summer drew to a close, with a warm breeze tinkling the crystal wind chimes on her porch, Nan was woken from her slumber. The doorbell was ringing. Tying a white cotton gown about her and slipping into a pair of cream slippers, she hastened down the hallway. The bell rang again, urgently, with a long 'RRRRRRR', as if someone had jammed the buzzer.

'Merciful saints! I'm coming!' she cried, though not so loudly as to awaken the Kitterlings. She squinted out into the night. There was no one there. No car in the drive, no one in the street beyond. She was about to return to bed, making a mental note to get a Hound electrician to fix the obviously faulty doorbell, when it rang again. This time when she flung open the door, she caught sight of a figure darting over the trimmed hedge and dashing off down the driveway. One of the local Tom-Kitterlings playing a prank, she thought.

Then she heard a strange muffled sound coming from the far end of the porch. She flicked on the light and went to investigate.

Marvin doubled back up the driveway and crouched behind the hedge. He could clearly see the old Cat Matron in curlers staring down at the bundle he had left by the pillar. He smirked at her startled gasp. Nothing could have prepared her for what she discovered.

She found herself staring at a large, grubby cardboard box – although this was not what concerned her. It was what was in the box that gave her pause. For, inside, taped and trussed like a Thanksgiving turkey was… a Houndling! Little Arthur Snout.

Immediately she could tell this was some kind of sick joke. The Houndling wore an amateurishly drawn mask, cut to the shape of a Cat face, in a crude attempt to cover his protruding snout. Nan wrinkled her nose at the distinctive odour of Hound, removed the mask, and peered at the frightened Houndling.

From the bushes bordering the Home, Marvin and his accomplice, Jasper, a thin whippet of a hound with moulting ears and a limp snout, watched with wicked delight.

'She'll toss him down those fancy stairs!' sniggered Marvin. 'Or maybe beat him with a broom till he's black and blue!'

The whole idea to truss up poor Lonely Dog and haul him, in the dead of night, across town to Catside, the forbidden neighbourhood, was of course Marvin's. His malicious prank to keep Lonely away from the Midsummer Festival had backfired spectacularly. Upon realizing that the slumbering Houndling at the back of the bus was nothing more than a stuffed suit, Bella had become incandescent with anger. She demanded Rolph turn the bus round and go back to Port Alveridge. But it was too late. The road leading to Marmalade Mountain was gridlocked. It was impossible to turn, let alone go back.

'There'll be other Blue Moons for little Snout to attend,' Rolph had said resignedly. Bella was inconsolable.

'He has a gift, Flannegan! A musical gift! If anyone should have been at the festival it was him.'

As punishment, Marvin spent the entire festival locked in the bus at the back of the sprawling car park. In the distance he could just hear the dulled sound of the festival, which made him seethe with rage. Once he was back at the Orphanage, his black mood was made even darker by a compulsory visit to the damaged woodshed in the company of Headmaster Flannegan and a bumprickle switch.

Marvin then set about planning one final coup de grâce for the little Hound – one last attempt to rid himself forever of his bête noire. He co-opted the spineless Jasper to push the ancient wheelbarrow, with Arthur bundled in it, all the way through Houndside, past the sleeping port, and on over the Juke River into Catside.

Being on the other side of the river was a drastically new experience for them both, so much so that their plan nearly unravelled. The streets on this side of town were frighteningly different from those on Houndside.

'Where's all the street stuff, Marvin?' Jasper asked nervously as he scoured the immaculate Feline avenues. 'This place gives me the willies. Them Cats will smell us for sure!'

'Stop snivelling!' snarled Marvin. 'Just keep pushing.'

As for Lonely, bound like a mummy in sticky tape, every painful bounce of that wheelbarrow was taking him further away from the only home he had ever known. Behind the crude Cat mask tears welled up in his eyes as he wondered what Marvin had in store for him.

He was soon to find out.

Marvin now watched and waited for his nasty jape to unfold. How he would laugh when the old puss screamed and then hurled the silly little Hound down the steps! His credentials as top dog would be restored.

But it was not to be.

Nan took one look at the desperate, pleading, nut-brown eyes, smiled a little half-smile and, to Marvin's surprise and horror, scooped up the bundle of Arthur Snout and took him inside. The door slammed behind her with a resounding bang.

Lonely gripped the edges of the white porcelain bath and peered through the steam with his big brown eyes. The kindly old Cat Matron had gone to fetch more soap and he felt it was safe to poke his head out of the bubbles and take a look around. The bathroom was enormous, with gilt mirrors lining one wall and the whitest, fluffiest towels he had ever seen hanging along another. There was a marble sink with gold taps shaped like Cats' tails and a shelf above it crammed with glass containers full of strange potions. The whole room smelled of vanilla pods.

He looked down at himself, his skin raw from the tape. Every inch of his body seemed to ache. For a moment he toyed with the idea of climbing out of the bath, tip-toeing across to find his clothes and shoes and sneaking out the back door to make his way back to Houndside. Then he remembered Marvin's parting words.

'Welcome to your new home, pussy-pants!' Marvin had hissed, tipping Lonely from the wheelbarrow on to the steps. 'Don't even think about coming back to Houndside, Cat lover!'

Lonely sank back into the steaming bathwater. Maybe going back wasn't such a good idea. Even if he could find his way to the Orphanage, what good would it do? He knew Marvin would follow through on his threats.

Suddenly Nan bustled in again, carrying an armful of soap and scrubbing brushes. Lonely plunged under the suds, only the top of his head and his snout visible, deeply embarrassed at being naked in a bath with a Cat standing over him.

She spoke sternly but with the hint of a smile beneath her whiskers. 'None of your Houndish nonsense, young pup. I have bathed more orphans than I care to remember and they all look exactly alike. Just as nature intended! So sit up and let me wash that filth off you.'

Rolling up her sleeves, Nan began to scrub the Houndling in places he didn't know existed.

'So then, what is your name and where do you come from?'

'Arthur Snout, but at the Orphanage they call me Lonely Dog.'

'Orphanage? Would that be Mr Flannegan's establishment?'

'Yes, ma'am.'

'You may call me Nan. And tell me why a Houndside orphan should be on my porch in the middle of the night, tied up and wearing a hideous Cat mask?'

'Marvin Bostock.'

'Would that be the same Mr Bostock who rang my bell and then scarpered as if the Devil himself were after him?'

'Yes, ma'am… I mean Nan.'

'And why would a fellow orphan treat his schoolmate in such a wicked way?'

Lonely took a deep breath and told her the whole story.

When he had finished she ordered him out of the bath, dried him briskly and wrapped him in a fluffy dressing gown.

'Well, young Mr Snout – or should I call you Lonely? – this evening you will be going nowhere but to bed. In the morning I shall make some enquiries and decide what is to be done with you. We are not accustomed to having young Hounds in this Home, not accustomed at all, so we will have to put you in the old caretaker's room for the night. It is clean and warm and out of the way. Follow me.'

She led him through the sparkling kitchen and out the back door, down the trim garden path, past neat rows of vegetables glowing in the moonlight, to a small whitewashed shed at the rear of the plot. Rakes and brooms lined one wall; against another there was a sagging but comfy bed piled high with crisp white pillows and a quilt. Next to it was a battered lamp on a simple table. The floor was bare but well scrubbed.

'You'll be comfortable in here for now, young Lonely,' Nan said, closing the sunflower-print curtains. 'I will have your suit and shoes cleaned and dried tomorrow. In the meantime, there's a pair of overalls on the hook in the corner.'

Then, to Lonely's surprise, she leaned down and kissed him on the nose.

'Goodnight,' she said, and closed the door.

Arthur sank on to the bed and pulled the lumpy quilt up to his snout. A hundred thoughts raced through his mind, but they would have to wait until morning. As soon as his head hit the starched pillow he fell into a deep sleep.

CHAPTER X

Catside on Slippered Feet

There are three things that will ruin a hound.
The first is the lust for power.
The second is the power of lust.
The third is a pistol to the head.
Of all three the latter is by far the most ruinous!

—Sir Vickers Barstudd III, Viscount of Byle.
From his book *How to Outwit Friends and
Infuriate People*, vol. 66

*I*n the dusty morning light, Lonely sat on the bed
in the caretaker's shed, tears flowing down his snout as
he read the letter in his hand. It was from Bella.

It was now two weeks since Marvin had dumped him on the porch of
the Alveridge Home for Cats. He had tried to keep his flagging spirits up,
to put on a brave smile. But today there was no bravery, no smiles.

Every day he had waited for news, hoping that Rolph, that someone,
would come for him. Once, passing by the kitchen window, he had overheard Nan talking on the telephone and the snatches of her side of the
conversation had made his ears prick up.

'…Yes, he is safe, for the moment…'

'…but my Home is no place for a Hound, I have Kitterlings to
consider…'

'…I understand that, but he should be with his own kind, back at the
Orphanage…'

'…What? Oh my Lord! I had no idea. Closed? Sold?…'

'…and what of Mr Flannegan?'

'…I see. Yes. Such a terrible shame…'

'…No, I think in the circumstances you should be the one to inform Arthur…'

As Nan hung up the receiver, brushing her hands over her starched white apron, Lonely had poked his head through the kitchen window.

'Was that Headmaster Flannegan?' he had asked.

Nan jumped. 'What did you hear?' she replied icily.

Lonely was taken aback. 'Nothing,' he lied, hanging his head.

'Good!' She continued, primly. 'At the Alveridge Home for Cats we do not creep around listening to conversations that do not concern us. That is something that only a—' She stopped, coughed. 'That is something we just do not do.'

But Lonely knew what she had really intended to say: 'That is something only a *Hound* would do!'

He had gone back to raking the leaves on the back lawn, face burning red with shame.

In the days that followed, he began to understand that there were indeed some things that Cats did not do. They did not rake leaves, chop firewood, weed or trim hedges. In fact nothing, it seemed, that might involve getting their soft hands dirty. Hounds on the other hand – or 'dogs' as he had heard the Kitterlings say – did all this and more. Old Hound trucks spluttered up to the trade entrance and dealt with all the odd jobs: fixing leaky pipes, changing burned-out light bulbs, taking away the garbage.

Nan had made it clear to Lonely that while things were being sorted out he was welcome to stay, but only under strict conditions. He was not to be seen inside the Home during classes or at mealtimes: his meals were served in the scullery, after the Kitterlings had eaten. His time was taken up with an exacting regime of chores – chopping, trimming, weeding, raking, painting, clipping – and though he was exhausted by the end of each day, Lonely was glad of the physical activity since it kept his mind off his fate. But at night, alone, he thought of nothing else. Mostly he thought of Kelzie and finally realized what everybody at the Orphanage had known for years: he was in love with the sweet Houndette with the button eyes and pigtails. Now he sat desultorily on the edge of his bed with the letter that Nan had slid under his door early that morning. Hungry for news of home, he had ripped it open. The writing was in Bella's unmistakable hand, but the words were far from comforting.

My dearest Arthur,

Thank the Good Lord that you are safe and sound at the Alveridge Home for Cats. I have been so worried for you.

When you disappeared we searched everywhere. It was not until the Matron at the Cats' Home called that we knew you were all right and that it was all my Marvin's doing. I feel so ashamed of him, my own flesh and blood!

He's been sent to the Trumaine Corrective Borstal for Hounds and, though it pains me to see him go, I know it is for the best.

But as one dark cloud passes, another blacker one appears.

The Orphanage is to be closed.

I can barely bring myself to write these words, dear Arthur.

Some days back, we were shocked to learn that our beloved Orphanage, which has stood for over two hundred years, is bankrupt and will be closed forthwith. I fair fainted when I heard.

But there is worse news still. It seems we have been bankrupted by dubious loans from a mysterious Cat financier, whom Mr Flannegan himself had been dealing with without the Board's knowledge. Though I am sure he meant well, it has backfired. The financier has foreclosed on the mortgage and we have all been forced to pack up and leave.

It has not been easy but I have managed to find homes for most of the destitute Houndlings. Times are tough and many Hounds are struggling to make ends meet. I have had to start taking in laundry down at the Port.

Unfortunately, Mr Flannegan has not fared well. In his shame at what he brought upon us all he began drinking down at the Port and I'm sorry to have to tell you he is now a shambling and broken Hound. I no longer recognize the upstanding Headmaster we all loved, and it seems he no longer recognizes us either.

After a great deal of persuading, I have managed to convince the Matron to allow you to stay at the Alveridge Home for Cats in the capacity of helper and kitchen-hand in return for lodging and tuition, at least for the time being.

But, dear Arthur, the time will come when you must decide on the road you will take. I know you will make wiser choices than my own Marvin.

Music is your gift, Arthur! Mr Flannegan always said that fate and music were conspiring to make a future for you; I can only hope and trust he was right. In the meantime, make the most of misfortune, learn what you can from Catside. Though they are a strange species, I have never felt as most Hounds do that they are foes.

Forgive my rambling and the tear stains that dot this missive.

Go well, my wee Hound. Angels brought you to me, they will surely guide you on your journey.

Bella Bostock

XXXXXXX

Lonely read it a tenth time, scouring the spaces between the words for the one piece of news that was not there. What had become of Kelzie?

He folded the letter and, as he had learned to do on his cold nights in the old Orphanage cellar, pushed his hurt and his tears into a dark part of his soul. There were chores to see to and Nan would want to know why they hadn't been done.

Any spare time after his chores he spent alone, practising the kitty-fiddle. After hearing his practice one day, Nan had allowed him to join her violin class in the grand music room, along with the younger Cats.

Things were so different to Houndside. He would find himself day-dreaming about Kelzie, thinking of Bronson, and reliving that night at the Green with Mr Flannegan. He would close his eyes, straining to remember the enchanting sound of Houndskiffle wafting over the Green so long ago.

CHAPTER XI

Powderkegs and Painkillers

I've got an ache in my heart
It won't go away
I remember the sunshine
How I wanted to stay.
But I'm too far from home
And I'm too long time gone
I've got tangled in troubles
My turning was wrong.

—Lonely Dog, 'Tangled in Troubles'.
Bootleg copy from early illicit broadcast

$\mathcal{S}$ummer had slipped its chain and the cold winds of
autumn now snapped like a rabid dog. A. K. Ruddegan
angrily tightened the cord of his velvet smoking
jacket. It was late, he was tired, the headache that had
bothered him all day was becoming a migraine.

He filled a crystal tumbler with tonic water and gulped it down. He
would have preferred something stronger but was expecting a telephone
call that would require a very clear head.

He padded across the plush carpet of his study and opened the door.

'Celia! Creme! Where are my damn painkillers?' he called out into
the vast marble atrium at the centre of his enormous mansion. From an
upstairs room came the blare of a gramophone. It assaulted his ears and
set his head pounding.

> I got me a suit and I got me a tie
>
> But the only time I'll wear 'em is the day I'm gonna die!

He scowled. 'Houndskiffle? In my house!' he thought.

'CELIA! Turn that infernal Hound racket off and help me find my painkillers!'

The bedroom door opened and the music poured out, causing Ruddegan to press his hands to his ears.

A young Cat stepped languidly out on to the landing. She was lean and tall with long, sinuous limbs. Her peroxide white hair was cropped in a mannish style and she wore tartan pyjamas, unbuttoned and knotted at her waist. Smoke wafted from her cigarillo.

'I haven't the faintest idea where your pills are,' she said, her smoky voice edged with a wry smile. 'I'm not your housekeeper!'

Ruddegan looked at her and some of his anger drained away.

'Well at least turn that dreadful Hound howling down or you'll have that old puss Nan phoning to complain we've woken her damn Kitterlings!'

He decided to turn on his Feline charm. 'Please, my darling Celia, be a dear and help your poor old grandfather find something for his splitting headache.'

Though she could be infuriating, Celia was his only granddaughter, and, since the death of his fifth wife, the only real family he had. His son, Celia's father, was a ne'er-do-well playboy who had squandered his substantial inheritance on loose Felines and even looser investments. Ruddegan had all but disowned him, but he had ensured his beloved Celia received the very best education: a Felinean finishing school, then further study at the Royal Pussonian Institute. His efforts has been to little avail, however, as Celia had simply tossed it all away and come sauntering back to Port Alveridge with not so much as a 'thank-you Puss Pop'.

Catside: Big Night Out

Puss Pop was what she had called him when long ago he would bounce her on his knee while scrutinizing spreadsheets. But thinking of the Kitterling she had been, he barely recognized her now. She had abandoned Feline lace and silk and now wore denim jeans and flannel work shirts. In fact, to his mounting alarm, she had started to absorb a disagreeable amount of Hound culture, however oxymoronic he thought the term. She played those infuriating Houndskiffle records day and night – Something Two-Fingers and His Hound-Something Band. He knew she snuck out at night to go to Houndside, to listen to the filthy slop the Hounds called blues.

Still, he loved her dearly, loved her as he did all his expensive possessions.

Suddenly the telephone rang. Hurrying back to his study, Ruddegan called back to her, 'Turn that music off, this is important.'

The telephone's ring seemed more insistent now, but it was not coming from the black-and-chrome handset on his desk. Checking that the curtains were tightly drawn, he hastily reached for an impressive bronze figurine on the bookcase – a statue of Felinicus the Merciless astride his war-horse – and depressed the sabre in the soldier's raised right paw.

There was a whir of cogs and wheels as the bookcase slid open with a well-oiled purr to reveal the source of the ringing: a magnificent radio transmitter with luminous valves and wire coils. A red light was flashing on its metal fascia. Ruddegan smoothed his silver whiskers, stroked his thin moustache, then cleared his throat nervously, put on the headphones and spoke into the mouthpiece.

'Mayor Colonel Ruddegan speaking,' he said tentatively.

There was a hiss of static, then a voice came through the headphones, distant yet chilling in its very closeness. It was a monotone voice, stripped of any colour. Like an undertaker giving a quotation.

'Mayor Ruddegan. Yes, I'd forgotten you had appointed yourself Mayor of Port Everidge.'

'Alveridge, Your Excellency.'

'What?'

'Port Alveridge, sir.'

'Everidge, Alveridge, what does it matter!'

Ruddegan was sweating profusely now, his head pounding painfully.

'I was speaking with my granddaughter—'

'Ah, yes. Celia. I heard she had abandoned her heritage. There have even been malicious rumours that she has – how to put it delicately – "gone to the dogs".'

Ruddegan felt a cold chill run up his spine.

'She is adjusting to life back home very well, Excellency. As you are aware, matters in Port Alveridge can be complicated, what with Hounds and Cats living so close—'

'Yes, yes!' the Voice interrupted, 'I am very aware. I am also aware that in spite of our repeated requests for you to keep those aforementioned Hounds of yours on a very short leash, you have failed.'

'H… how so, Your Excellency?' Ruddegan stammered, blood draining from his face. 'If you're referring to the Blue Moon phenomenon, I can hardly be blamed. Those primitive Hounds are virtually uncontrollable when it appears.'

'I am not referring to the Blue Moon – although production figures for the Cannery during that period were markedly lower than acceptable. I am referring to that swinehound the Baron of Beaconsfield and to the Hound Resistance movement he is marshalling under your very nose at his Beaconsfield estate.'

'But, Excellency, the Baron is an old windbag, nothing more – all bark and no bite!'

'He may have no bite,' the Voice climbed a shrill, deathly octave, 'but his bark is heard all over Alveridgea and beyond, as far as Felinea and other lands. He has erected a powerful radio transmitter on a hill above his castle from where he broadcasts anti-Felinean propaganda to all who would listen.'

'Excellency, I—'

'Shut up and listen!' The Voice cut him off. 'You will put a stop to these broadcasts and indeed the Baron himself! He is old, but he is no fool. We have met before, on the battlefield. Do I make myself clear, *Mayor* Ruddegan, or do you need special "assistance" in your doggy backwater?'

'No, no, Excellency! I will take care of it. In fact I already have the means to do exactly that. Leave it to me and—'

The red light stopped flashing, the line suddenly a continual hiss of static.

Ruddegan wiped his brow and waited for his heart to stop pounding.

He pressed the bronze sabre and the bookcase slid shut.

After he had poured himself a very large gin, he sat back in his leather armchair and pondered his next move. The Powers represented by the Voice were real and very frightening; he held his position in Port Alveridge by their consent. Everything he had achieved, every penny he had clawed, every rung he had climbed, could be stripped away at a single word from the Powers. His eyes burned blood-red. He would not allow this to happen, not if it meant strangling every last Hound who got in his way! He had told His Excellency that he had the means to deal with the Baron – and he had. He knew just the Hound.

But where was the useless old drunk to be found at this time of night?

CHAPTER XII

Music and Mayhem

I woke up this morn
With them blue-jean-blues
Can't patch up my heart
where our love wore thru.
So find yourself a needle
Fetch your Momma's thread
Git to sewing, baby, while I lie here in bed

—Buckshot Huxley, from his debut album
Sixteen Ways To Strip a Carburetor

*C*elia opened her balcony door and stepped out, lit a cigarillo and blew smoke at the stars. From her bedroom came the mournful cadences of a Missin' Tooth Memphis record that perfectly matched her mood.

> I got everything but nothing
>
> Travelled far and never left
>
> I got healed but now I'm hurtin'
>
> Got told the answer but I'm deaf

Celia knew all there was to know about music. At the Royal Pussonian Institute she'd attended operas that soared and thundered, roared and wailed yet did not express emotion as perfectly as this simple blues song. She picked up the silver harmonica that lay on the table by the door and blew a few tentative notes, joining in the chorus.

> Got me a long road to travel
>
> Got me a stone in my shoe

Got me a bag full of nothing
Got me an ocean full of blue.

Her grandfather detested the harmonica – 'drone-whistle' he called it – and perhaps that was why she had bought it down at the Green. He hated her going there too. 'You have a gift for music, Celia,' he would chide, 'why waste it on that Hound-piffle they play at Revellers Green?' But Celia thrilled to the sounds and the atmosphere at the Green. They moved her in ways that startled and sometimes even frightened her, those songs that cut so deep and yet felt so good.

The record ended, the needle scratching and hissing. Celia was about to step inside and flip it over when she heard an intriguing sound drifting across the garden below. Leaning over the balcony, she peered into the darkness and listened.

It was creeping over the wall from the nearby Alveridge Home for Cats: the beautiful timbre of a stringed instrument – not a guitar and not a violin, but something in between. Maybe a mandolin, she thought, as she slipped on her dressing gown, swung over the balcony railings and climbed down the ivy trellis with practised ease. She followed the sound of the music through the lush garden, past marble statuary and fancifully trimmed hedges, until she came to the high stone wall at the bottom. Celia hiked her gown around her waist and began to climb. Dropping down the other side, she found herself in an orderly, practical plot full of tidy rows of vegetables and compost bins. In the corner, partially hidden by an overhanging Nickleberry tree, was a white garden shed. The window was ajar and yellow light glowed through the drawn curtains. The music was coming from within.

Celia peeped through the window, expecting to find one of Nan's Kitterlings plucking surreptitiously inside. What she saw instead first shocked then thrilled her: it was a young Hound, sitting on the edge of a bed, playing the strangest instrument she had ever seen.

∾

Lonely adjusted the tuning pegs and ran his fingers over the strings. The sound he produced was startling and different from anything he had heard or played before.

Nearly five years had passed since Bella's letter and the seasons had blurred together like names left in the sand for the tide to wash away. Though the Kitterlings at the Cat Home were friendly, and their unabashed curiosity at all things Hound amused him, he spent most of the time by himself. Nan kept him busy, and he had the calloused hands of a working Hound to show for it. Nor were these the only changes he'd noticed: his voice, once higher than other Hounds his age, had deepened and burred. He found it more difficult to hit the top notes, but he liked the rumble of the lower ones better.

Nan had caught him singing one day while he was scrubbing rubbish bins. She didn't normally approve of that kind of behaviour, but on this occasion she'd paused and given him a strange look. Lonely had blushed, mumbling an apology, but to his surprise Nan had told him to carry on. She'd looked out through the trees and muttered an old Cat proverb so quietly Lonely could only just hear: 'The sap is flowing, the tree is growing, what fruit it bears is beyond our knowing.'

The instrument he now cradled he had fashioned with his own hands.

When Nan had asked him to dispose of some clutter and broken kitty-fiddles from the music room, Lonely's eyes had lit up. He had no intention of burning the curious violins. Instead, he'd taken them back to his room and spent many long nights painstakingly cannibalizing the tuning pegs, strings and necks and building something that looked and felt like Rolph's Alveridgean five-string; though the body had the distinctive look of a fiddle, the fretboard was longer, with scrolled violin tuning pegs at the head. He had discarded the bow and lovingly sanded and varnished the instrument until it glowed.

Now, he strummed the strings and coughed once. Then, reading the lyrics he'd scribbled on a fertilizer leaflet over many long and lonely nights, he began to sing. It was for Kelzie, and as he sang his eyes shone.

When I hold your hand
Stars collide
The world is new
And all that's left
Is me with you

When I kiss your lips
Angels weep
Demons flee
And all that's left
Is you with me.

So hold my hand and kiss me long
I'll reach for you with my song

Together we will climb the hill

And forever be together still.

When I see your smile

Comets fly

The Moon turns blue

And all Time and Space

Is me and you

He stopped, fumbled for another chord. Suddenly a voice from the window startled him and he almost dropped his guitar.

'You must love her very much.'

Alarmed, he turned, worried he had woken Nan. Instead he saw a tall female Cat with cropped white hair, the like of whom he'd never encountered before.

'You must love her very much,' she said again in a smoky voice. 'The girl in your song.'

Lonely set down the instrument and awkwardly approached the Cat at the window. 'I did, I mean I do love her. Who are you?'

'Celia,' she replied, as if this were explanation enough. 'Let me in, it's freezing out here.'

Lonely opened the door uncertainly and Celia breezed in as if they were old friends.

'Fancy finding a Hound down the garden path!' She smiled. 'I heard you playing and came for a look.' She picked up Lonely's instrument admiringly. 'Where'd you get it?'

'I made it.'

'You made this?' she said, each syllable carefully enunciated. 'May I?' she asked, sitting on the bed and resting the guitar on her lap.

'Sure,' he mumbled. 'You might need to—'

'Adjust the G string? I got it,' Celia replied, expertly twanging the string and twiddling the tuning peg at the same time.

'You play guitar?' he asked. 'I didn't think, I mean…'

'You didn't think Cats played guitar?' She laughed at his discomfort. '*They* don't; *I* do.'

She played a riff, her long fingers working the fretboard with ease. 'I learned from a blind Hound on the Green.'

She started a tune and Lonely immediately exclaimed, 'That's a Van Trong song!'

'Yep!' She smiled. '"It Just Ain't Right", from his *Protest Songs To Dance To* album. You know it?'

'*Boss Man you can beat me, you can even dock my pay…*' Lonely sang.

'*But Boss Man you get ready 'cause here comes Judgement Day…*' Celia sang right back.

'*It just ain't right,*' they sang together.

When the song ended, the questions started:

'Do you know so-and-so?'

'Sure I know him – how about…'

And so they talked on into the night – and into the many nights that followed.

Lonely found himself eagerly waiting for Celia to appear with her silver harmonica so they could jam into the small hours.

One evening she lugged a heavy box with her, which he helped haul over the wall. It contained a gramophone and a selection of Houndskiffle and blues. Together they listened to the scratchy records until the night was almost done. Then, as the last song died and Lonely's humming lingered on the air, Celia asked him about life back in the Orphanage.

It was the first time they had talked about themselves, their past. Lonely knew only that Celia was from next door, 'staying with my grandfather for a while, until I get myself together', whatever that meant. But in their long evenings he had begun to like this strange, almost un-Feline Cat who shared his musical tastes and in whom he sensed a loneliness and a restlessness equal to his own.

So when she asked, he told her everything, the words coming in a torrent: his strange arrival at the Orphanage in a shoebox, Marvin's bullying, dear Bella, big brother Bronson, his first trip to the Green with old Rolph, and Kelzie, sweet Kelzie. Finally he told her how he came to be here at the Cat Home.

'Unbelievable,' she whispered as if to herself. 'Why didn't you go back to the Orphanage, to Kelzie?'

Lonely took Bella's letter from his pocket and handed it to her. When she had finished reading it, Celia stood up, tears brimming in her emerald eyes, and hugged him! Then, without a word, she disappeared out the door and over the wall, leaving Lonely wondering if he'd said too much, and thinking how little he understood the female of any species.

∽

The following night and the night after that, Lonely sat up late waiting for Celia to return. On the third night, when it was clear she wasn't coming, he decided to go and find her. He slung his guitar over his shoulder, and – ignoring Nan's golden rule – climbed the wall.

The garden on the other side was dark and scented. Lonely followed the path of crushed shells towards the huge mansion that loomed white and imposing in the moonlight. Every light in the vast house seemed to be on, but he could not see Celia or even guess which of the many rooms was hers. He marvelled at the opulence, the marble statues that lined the colonnaded verandas, the tinkling fountains, the crystal chandeliers. Celia's grandfather must be a very wealthy Cat, he thought.

Suddenly he heard voices and instinctively stepped back into the shadows, peering upwards. Through an open bay window on the second floor he could see a large room hung with heavy gilt-framed paintings, stuffed boars' heads and antique hunting rifles. From within came a gruff, angry voice, which Lonely assumed belonged to Celia's grandfather. He recognized Celia's voice too, sounding hurt and wild. Lonely edged towards the creeper-covered wall of the house and listened.

'It *was* you, wasn't it!' cried Celia.

'Who told you about that, Celia? I have a right to know!' her grandfather demanded angrily.

'Answer me!' she screamed.

'Calm down! The whole neighbourhood can hear.'

'Who cares! I *want* them to hear. My grandfather throws defenceless orphans out on to the streets so he can line his filthy pockets!'

'What do you care, Celia?' he shouted back. 'You were happy to take my "filthy" money when it paid for everything! The fancy education, the cars, the clothes…'

'I didn't realize it was all paid for with blood money from the Hound-side Orphanage!'

'They were just Hounds! Dogs! They *live* on the streets!' he snarled.

Lonely heard Celia screech. Glass shattered on the marble floor.

'They were helpless *puppies!*' she cried. 'Houndlings!'

Lonely's ears stood on end, his heart began to thump.

'Celia! I order you to shut your mouth or I'll have no choice but to—'

'To what?' she challenged. 'Get your Tom thugs to rough me up a little, toss me out on the streets? What would the good citizens of Port Alveridge think of their precious mayor then?'

Lonely staggered backwards, his snout trembling. Celia's grandfather was none other than A. K. Ruddegan himself: the immoral 'Cat financier' Bella had mentioned in her letter, the one who had ruined Rolph Flannegan and seen Kelzie cast out into the cold!

There was the sound of a vicious slap. Celia yelped.

'You ungrateful little tramp!' Ruddegan yelled. 'I'll teach you the meaning of respect. Maybe I *should* throw you out into the gutter with the filthy Hounds you love so much—'

Ruddegan's tirade didn't get any further. He raised his hand a second time but before he could deliver the blow Lonely had scaled the creeper trellis, his head filled with a red cloud of rage, and come hurtling through the bay window. Celia, who lay sprawled and sobbing on the floor, looked up in shock.

'Lonely?'

'Who are *you?*' hissed Ruddegan, whirling like a startled snake, hand still raised.

'I'm one of the Houndlings you threw into the gutter!' snarled Lonely, baring his teeth, guitar case still slung on his shoulder. He stood between Celia, prone on the carpet, and Ruddegan. 'Never lay a hand on her again! NEVER!' he growled.

Ruddegan took a step back, feigning contrition, then suddenly sprang for a side table, grabbing a heavy crystal ashtray. He came swinging at Lonely, catching him off guard, striking the Hound's raised arm with a sickening thwack. Lonely crashed to the floor, holding his shattered limb above his head, and tried to ward off the rain of blows. Blood and fur splattered everywhere. He was sinking into a painful black hole…

Celia sprang to her feet and with a desperate charge managed to knock her startled grandfather backwards into a cabinet of chinaware, which shattered into a thousand pieces.

She raced to Lonely's side. Blood soaked the carpet and the small Hound was lying deathly still, his cracked guitar case beside him.

'Lonely! Lonely!… Are you all right?'

Suddenly there came the unmistakable sound of a gun being cocked.

She whirled around in horror to see Ruddegan standing over her with a triple-barrelled blunderbuss that he had snatched off the wall. A box of cartridges spilled across the desk. The old Cat was wild-eyed and crazy, adrenaline electrifying his silver whiskers.

'My great-grandfather used to shoot vermin Hounds with this,' he snarled. 'And I'm only too glad I could keep up the family tradition! Now get out of my way, Celia!' He levelled the wicked-looking weapon at the helpless Hound.

In a flash Celia grabbed the cracked ashtray, still wet with Lonely's blood, and hurled it at Ruddegan. As he parried it with his blunderbuss, Celia sprang again, grabbing the barrels and forcing them away from Lonely.

There was a deafening explosion.

Lonely struggled to his feet, his head spinning, blood still pouring from his arm and head. Through stinging eyes, his ears ringing from the gun blast, he saw Celia standing over the slumped body of her grandfather. The ancient blunderbuss lay smoking at her feet.

Viscous blood was oozing from a hole in the old Cat's shoulder and spreading over his velvet smoking jacket. Ruddegan's mouth was opening and closing like a goldfish, but only gurgling noises emerged.

From outside came the sound of angry shouts and boots pounding up marble stairs.

'It just went off!' Celia cried, her eyes wide with shock. 'I didn't mean to shoot him!'

There was a violent hammering on the door.

Celia snapped her head round. 'Come on, Lonely! I've got to get you away from here – *now*!'

He yowled as she grabbed his injured arm with one hand and his guitar with the other and propelled him through the bay window.

'Where are we going?' he whimpered as they crashed to the lawn below.

'Houndside – the Green!' she shouted.

Lonely gasped for air. His world was spinning, his legs buckling under him.

'We'll take my car!' Celia cried, just as Ruddegan's Toms appeared at the window.

CHAPTER XIII

Carousels and Party-crashers

Let it hereby be Noted that under Section VIII, Article 178
of the Port Alveridge By-Laws and Regulatory Statutes,
all Motorbike Gangs, Clubs and Affiliated Groups
are forthwith Forbidden, under Threat of Prosecution
and Imprisonment without Trial, to Ride aforesaid
Motorbikes, Houndsters and Motorized Cycles in a
Noisy, Disorderly, Raucous or Dangerous Manner.

—Port Alveridge Town Council Ordinance

Get screwed!

—Bronson, Leader of the Howlers Motorcycle Gang

$\mathcal{F}$or the second time in his life Lonely was being driven to Revellers Green at high speed and in style.

Celia had accelerated the Meowitzer 700 convertible out of the garage and smashed through the gate-house barrier, burning rubber as she roared down the sleepy streets of North Tolleston. Behind them, a posse of armed security Toms gave swift pursuit, though they were unable to shoot at the fleeing Hound because of the risk of hitting the Mayor's granddaughter.

'Do you think I killed him?' Celia asked, her sad eyes reflected in the dashboard light.

'No, it was just a flesh wound. He was still breathing when we left.' Lonely grimaced, clutching his own bleeding arm.

They sped down Sunset Boulevard, past bars and cafés still buzzing with late-night drinkers.

'Why are we going to the Green?' Lonely asked, hearing the distant sound of Houndskiffle.

'The Howlers.'

Lonely struggled to sit up. 'The Howlers?'

'You said you knew one of them, some "big brother" sort of guy.'

'Bronson?'

'Yeah, Bronson. I'm guessing he'll be the only one who'll be able to get you out of town. You gotta leave this place… Fast!'

'Leave town? Why?'

She didn't answer at first, ploughing through a red light.

He looked across at her, her features flash-ing, in the flare of the passing streetlights, but she didn't turn, still focused on keeping the car on the road. Her eyes were wet with tears and leaking black mascara, yet ablaze with an intensity that frightened the wounded Hound.

'I shot my grandfather, it was an accident and I could have killed him, but he won't blame *me*. Whatever I've done, I'm still his granddaughter. He'll pin the blame on *you*, Lonely, and no one will doubt the Mayor's word. That's why you've got to leave town right away. Or he'll have you arrested and sent "Upriver".'

'Upriver' was local slang for Ruddegan's notorious prison, a prison ship moored upriver at Fever Creek. Many a Hound was

Bronson Bostony
LEADER OF THE HOWLERS

dragged there in chains, but few ever returned, and those that did spoke in terrified tones of a teeming hellhole, guarded by sadistic Toms.

At Revellers Green, Celia jammed on the brakes, swinging the convertible up on to the kerb, almost knocking over a row of Howler motorbikes tethered like steel stallions.

She flung open the car door, grabbed him by his sleeve.

'Come on, Lonely, we've got to find Bronson!'

They raced across the Green, past the minstrels and carnival folk. Bronson proved easy to find: he stood snout and shoulders above the other bikers in their leathers and studs, their jackets emblazoned with the crossed bones and Hound skull that was the Howlers' emblem. Despite his young age, Bronson was indisputably the leader of the pack. He was delivering a rousing speech, his voice rumbling like morning thunder.

'We Hounds have been riding bikes, cruising the streets, and howling out loud for generations. We set our own timetable, sleep when we want, eat and drink as we please. We serve no boss, clock or timesheet, bow before no Cat. No damn pussy politician will ever change what was never meant to be changed! Howl On!' He raised a massive fist and punched the air.

The bikers erupted in wild cheers and guttural hoots of 'Bron-son! Bron-son! Bron-son!' as their leader ripped the cap off a bottle of Wilks with his teeth and swallowed the contents in one gulp.

Suddenly he spotted Celia pushing her way through the hairy circle of Howlers. The bikers were about to forcibly eject her, when he raised his hand.

'Let the Cat through! She's either very stupid or very brave – which is it, Cat?'

Celia stood before him, gasping, 'It's Lonely! He needs your help! Get him out of town – *tonight!*' She pointed behind her.

Lonely was staggering up the path clutching his bloodied arm, his guitar strapped to his back. He smiled weakly, faltered and fell.

'LONELY?' In a bound, Bronson was by the wounded Hound's side, scooping him up in his huge hands. 'What happened? Who did this?' he snarled.

'There isn't time!' Celia cried, gesturing at the road surrounding the Green. 'They've found us!'

Ruddegan's Toms were spilling out of long black sedans, brandishing clubs and shotguns, running, shouting, circling the park.

Bronson's eyes smouldered like a fuse about to ignite. 'HOWLERS!' he boomed, 'LET'S RIDE!'

Celia grabbed him. 'The Toms have the exits covered, we'll never make it out of here…'

A smile rippled across the big Hound's face. 'Create me a diversion, boys, and make them Toms hurt bad!'

The Howlers whooped and charged en masse towards the approaching Toms. The air filled with the crunching of knuckle-dusters on bone, boot on flesh.

Bronson ran, with Lonely still held close and Celia in hot pursuit, towards the far side of the Green, where two tiny Houndlings were sitting astride a large motorbike, one of many on the colourful merry-go-round. Celia stared at it, bewildered.

'Sorry, young 'uns,' barked Bronson and the Houndlings clambered down and dashed away. Bronson pulled hard at the securing pins and deftly whirled the bike from the carousel.

'Always have a back-up plan,' Bronson explained. 'We keep old Growler here in case one of us needs to make a getaway.'

He climbed on to the bike, settling Lonely on the pillion behind him. 'We'll be past the Toms and down the road before they know what's happened!'

'Where will you take him?'

'To the Juke Hounds. He'll be among friends there – *Hound* friends.'

The Howlers

'I was his friend,' Celia said tremulously as Bronson hung Lonely's faithful five-string on his shoulder.

Bronson didn't answer but nodded and kicked the starting pedal. In a blast of smoke and flame the bike took off through the crowd, the front wheel rearing into the air as though about to soar skywards. With the howl of a hundred skinned Cats they thundered along the Boulevard.

'Mr Flannegan?' Lonely mumbled, still groggy, clinging to Bronson. 'Are we going home?'

Bronson laughed, but his eyes were set like two welded rivets.

'Yeah, Lonely, we're going home. We're going to the Shipwoods!'

CHAPTER XIV

Escape to Blizzard Valley

This is the Faith
Faith of our Fathers
This is the Sound
The Sound of the Hound
These are Our Voices
Raised in these Mountains
Nowhere else can this Sound be Found!

— 'Hymns of Faith and Moonshine',
from the *Juke Hounds Hymnal*, vol. 89

*T*he Shipwoods were much more than the principal
mountain range of Greater Alveridgea. So steeped were they
in legend that to say someone had 'gone Shipwood' was to
say they had fled rational society and lost their mind. For
the Shipwoods inhabited not only the dark, cold corner of
Alveridgea, but the dark, cold corner of Hound imagination.

Here, among mountains hooded with snow and ice, the sun afforded
only fleeting benediction as the wind howled through the dark valleys
like a tortured soul begging for redemption.

But there was no redemption for those who had *gone Shipwood*.

Despite the barren landscape – or because of it – some Hounds had
made the Shipwoods their home. They were known as the Juke Hounds
(and as 'crazy fanatical inbreeds' or 'Cat-hating Doom-sayers', depending
on which bar you drank in).

It is true that the Jukes had fled to the mountains because of persecu-
tion, and equally true that they were also escaping restrictive liquor laws.

In the Shipwoods they found the perfect place to practise their peculiarly incendiary faith and distil their peculiarly inflammatory Houndhooch.

Devoid of any flat land to crop, and hostile to most plant life apart from hanging moss and swamp ferns, the mountains gave nothing and expected less. Yet from the Shipwoods' stony breast the cunning Jukes managed to squeeze one valuable resource – coal. With this vast trove of black rock, hideously difficult to mine, the Jukes powered their industry and their faith, their distilleries and their music.

The Juke Hounds were led by a firebrand, old as the mountains themselves, named Brother Jeroboam. Standing over six feet tall, with white whiskers that swept back from his snout like the wings of an avenging angel, his eyes blazed with coal-fired zeal. Brother Jeroboam did not *practise* religion: he was, as he often reminded his fervent congregation, an *expert*. He preached the vilification of all things Cat – though the word 'Cat' did not exist in the Jukes' lexicon, the preferred term being 'moggrels' or, Brother Jeroboam's particular favourite, 'vermin-puss'.

It was Brother Jeroboam's great-grandfather who had originally led the Hounds to the Shipwoods, and it was he who had set down the twin bulwarks of their faith: 'Heavy Toil and Heavy Music'.

If the Juke Hounds had fled Port Alveridge with nothing but the shirts on their backs (and the whisky in their pockets), they had also brought Hound music. Over the decades, traditional Houndskiffle and Working-Hound Blues had transformed into something infinitely more reflective of their bleak environment: into a coal-fired kick-in-the-guts industrial sound that the Jukes called 'Heavy' and Brother Jeroboam called 'Hound Sound'.

Whatever name you gave it, it rocked – literally.

Nothing summed up this unique sound and its associated faith better than the founding hymn penned by Brother Jeroboam's great-grandfather:

Brother Jukes we are Gathered

Mountain High and Mines so Deep

Sworn upon our Righteous Promise

From Vermin-Puss our Sound to Keep!

'Them vermin-puss have infected Greater Alveridgea with their moggrel ways!' Brother Jeroboam boomed every week from the pulpit of his granite cathedral in the gloomy town of Molars Post. A congregation of bearded Hounds, stained with coal-dust, would clap and howl their approval as outside the cold mist swirled like an incantation. 'They have corrupted that most precious of all things: our music! They have tainted it with their moggrel muck! It is the Devil's music, and our weak brothers back in Port Alveridge have allowed it to happen right under their snouts!' More thunderous endorsement and howling.

Mick the Bass Hound

'But we have set ourselves apart! We are the keepers of the True Music! We are the creators of the Juke Box!'

At this point he would invariably whirl around, execute a flourish worthy of a ringmaster and throw back a black curtain. This revealed a gigantic metal box complete with throbbing valves and greasy pneumatic pistons that were driven by the sooty steam engine standing alongside it. The congregation would fall silent.

'Within this sacred Juke Box, created through hard toil and Juke ingenuity, are the precious obsidian discs engraved with our sacred Sound!'

Jeroboam would grasp the metal lever and plunge it down, crying, 'Thus, my brothers, our music will never be forgotten, for we will sing it oft and we will sing it loud as it was meant to be sung!'

With a mechanical whirr, a black disc would start to spin. There would be a crackle of harsh static then a blast of sound so forceful it would blow the whiskers of every Hound backwards. The thunderous bass would boom like a sledgehammer, the guitar riff exploding like a chainsaw murderer locked in a tin shed.

Then, in a show of raucous unity, the Juke Hounds would stomp their steel-capped boots and mosh. As their hardened bodies slammed against each other in pure, belligerent joy, their husky voices strained by coal-dust but powered by the passion of their faith, they would roar as one beneath the throbbing sanctum sanctorum of their faith – the Juke Box.

It was to this strange and fearsome world that Bronson and Lonely were now speeding.

CHAPTER XV

A Weasel Named Jenny La Rue

I've been running on empty for so long
It'd take an ocean to fill my tank
But darlin' you can check my oil
Maybe give my heart a crank

—Lonely Dog, 'Blizzard Valley Blues'

*C*logged with snow and ice, the road was narrowing
like an old Hound's artery. Bronson had been riding east
for over two hours, through small, dark hamlets, past
farmland shadowy in the moonlight. But now the road rose
steeply, the air growing colder with every mile. Up ahead,
silhouetted against the moon, loomed the Shipwoods.

Lonely was still slumped against the big Hound's back. He hadn't moved
for a long time and Bronson worried that his charge had lost a lot of blood.
He checked his mirrors. The Toms had yet to catch up. He'd shaken off
the black sedan when he'd fishtailed down a gravel track and his pursu-
ers had smashed into a maple tree. But they'd be back on his trail soon.
It wouldn't be difficult to work out where he was headed, but Bronson
knew no Cat would enter Juke territory without reinforcements.

Suddenly his headlight caught a shack by the side of the road. A single
yellow light flickered on the sagging porch and out front, rusty as a
trawler's deck, stood an ancient fuel-pump. Bronson pulled to a stop, the
big bike shuddering with gratitude.

He gently lifted Lonely off the pillion seat and helped him up the rickety steps to the ragged fly-screened door. A faded sign hanging from a piece of tatty string read: 'Blizzard Valley Store 'N' Fuel – Closed For Winter'. Bronson banged on the door with his boot. There came a shuffling sound from inside, then a voice, all phlegm and gums.

'We're closed! Can't you read? Come back in summer.'

'Toothless Bob? That you?'

There was a pause, then the voice said, 'Who wants to know?'

'Me, Bronson of the Howlers! Open the door! Now open this damned door!'

Chains rattled, bolts slid back, then the door opened a crack. A face peered through the fly-screen. Hoary whiskers hung like swamp moss from the old Hound's crooked snout. His eyes were red rimmed and his tongue constantly moistened his toothless gums. In his arthritic hands he clutched a double-barrelled shotgun.

'That really you, Bronson?' he queried, squinting so hard his eyeballs disappeared. 'Who's the little fella? He don't look so good.'

'I need fuel and bandages,' said Bronson urgently.

'Fuel and bandages,' repeated the old Hound, licking his gums. 'You in some kinda trouble?'

'Toms,' Bronson said, casting his eyes back towards Port Alveridge.

'Toms?' gummed Toothless Bob, throwing open the door and ushering them indoors with the barrel of his gun, then poking his old head out into the night. 'They comin' this way?'

'Soon,' was all Bronson said. Then, 'How about them bandages and maybe some hot water.'

The old Hound slammed the door shut and shuffled past them into the shack's gloomy interior. He lit a kerosene lantern and hung it on a nail, illuminating the cluttered store and its long counter piled with packs of spark-plugs, chewing tobacco and dusty postcards. At one end was an ancient till, at the other a coffee pot of chipped enamel smeared with oily fingerprints. At the far side of the room, on a lumpy couch covered with old newspapers and dog-eared car magazines, a pet weasel lay curled asleep.

Toothless tipped the papers and magazines on to the dusty floor and shooed away the startled weasel.

'You can lay the little fella down here's a while. I'll go boil some water.' Bronson tenderly laid the little Hound on the couch.

'He got him a name?'

'They call him Lonely Dog.'

'And what do you call him then?'

'I call him Friend. Now get that water boiling, Toothless, and fetch those bandages, 'cause them Toms could be calling soon.'

Toothless gave a grim, gummy smile.

'Like a see 'em try! All they'll get is a tail full of buckshot!'

Lonely sat up. His arm ached. He vaguely remembered the midnight ride from the Green: clinging to Bronson, the roar of the bike, the cold wind blasting his ears back. He looked around the cluttered shack. Something caught his eye. It was a weasel, sitting at the end of the couch, peering indignantly at him.

'Bronson?' he called, not taking his eyes off the weasel.

A figure emerged from the back of the store, carrying a cup of steaming, tar-black coffee.

'You awake, fella? You been 'sleep 'bout five hours. Oh, don't pay no mind to Jenny La Rue, she's just miffed that you took her spot!'

Lonely rubbed his forehead, still trying to take in his surroundings.

'Where's Bronson?'

'Gone,' Toothless Bob replied, noisily slurping the scalding coffee.

'Gone? Where?'

'Gone in a hurry, that's where. Them Toms came lookin' for you 'bout an hour after he brought you here.'

'Where's here?' Lonely interrupted, still trying to clear the cottonwool from his brain.

'Blizzard Valley, last fuel station afore the Shipwood Mountains. I'm Toothless Bob and—'

'The Shipwoods!' cried Lonely, as it all came back to him. 'I remember now! We were headed for the Shipwoods…'

'—he pulled in here to tend your wounds, you was bleedin' like a stuck pig,' continued Toothless. 'Then we got news the Toms was heading up here.'

'News?'

The old Hound pointed to an even older radio transmitter on a shelf behind the counter. 'Ain't got no fancy telephones up here, but we do got radio transmitters. News travels faster than a cat fart in a tornado! One of our brother Jukes seen the Toms' convoy down Tippleton Creek, headed this way, and sent out the warning. Soon as Bronson heard it, he reckoned to head 'em off, make like a decoy towards Beaconsfield.

He had to leave you behind, little fella, 'cause you were still asleep and hurtin'. I promised him I'd get you to Molars Post safe, just as soon as you were feelin' better.'

'Molars Post?' asked Lonely.

'That's the main Juke township, way up in the mountains. Ain't no damn Cat ever gonna get you up there, no sir, 'cause that's Brother Jeroboam's territory.'

Lonely slumped back on the couch and wondered where Bronson was right now. And what about Celia?

If only he hadn't climbed that garden wall. If only he hadn't stuck his snout into her argument with Ruddegan. All this was *his* doing! The guilt felt like a rock on his chest. It seemed wherever he went he caused only pain and trouble to everyone around him – Celia, Bronson, old Rolph, Bella, Kelzie…

'You look like you seen a ghost, little fella,' Toothless said. 'Reckon you best get some more rest.'

He took the kerosene lantern and shuffled out of the room, turning at the door to say something, but Lonely was already asleep.

'He got the weight of somethin' heavy on his little shoulders, that's a fact!' mumbled the old Hound and quietly closed the door, leaving Lonely to the darkness and his nightmares.

In his dreams, Lonely was running down an endless highway, away from those he'd hurt, from his past, away to the mountains. In the dream, the past was just a memory; in the dream he never came back.

CHAPTER XVI

Rickety Rails to Freedom Swamp

Toothless Bob got a jar of 'shine
Got it from a friend of mine
Made from a hidden still
Still hidden in them hidden hills.
Still makin' 'shine , still makin' 'shine
Makin' it since before time
Makin' shine, makin' shine
Drink it up! You've still got time!

—Billy-Rick & Mortis and The Swamp Stompers,
'Swamp Swigging Singalong for Children'

*J*enny La Rue was the first to hear it, the sound of tyres crunching gravel, but no engine. The sound of someone approaching who didn't want to be observed.

Outside, the mountain mist swirled and a freezing rain painted the bleak landscape bleaker. The Blizzard Valley Store was sandbagged with snow drifts. The weak kerosene lamp, glowing through the frosted window, was the only colour in a land of white. Inside, Lonely sat on a cane chair by the radio transmitter, twiddling the knobs with his cold fingers. A sooty pot-belly stove crackled as Toothless Bob stirred a dented pan of breakfast bacon and beans.

'You getting' anything?' he enquired as he tested the beans.

Lonely kept fiddling, then suddenly a burst of static and the sound of twanging banjos and skiffle boards.

'Now that's more like it!' Toothless shouted gleefully, tapping his stirring spoon on the edge of the pan. 'Some Houndhooch Blues to start the day with! Get out that guitar of yours and join on in!'

Lonely reached for his guitar and began to pick along with the Hound-hoochers on the crackling radio.

> Got me some whisky from my mama's still
>
> She got it from my granddaddy's will
>
> He got it from a man he killed
>
> Stealing whisky from my mama's still!

Into the second verse and Lonely was now thumping his foot on the floor, adding chords and riffs that made Toothless shake his head in astonishment. The little fella sure could play!

In the months since his nephew had burst into his store with the bleeding Hound in his big arms, Toothless had nursed the youngster back to health as best he could. When the snow eased, he would fire up his old pick-up and head up to Molars Post and the Jukes, just as he'd promised Bronson. Toothless had always felt a mite guilty that he hadn't raised his nephew himself, after Bronson's parents died in the train crash down at Ravensport Junction. But, as the Orphanage headmaster – what was his name again, Finnegin? Flannegan! – had said, Blizzard Valley Store 'N' Fuel was no place to raise a Houndling. Besides, Bronson had turned out just fine.

'And now I got's me another little fella to take care of.' He smiled to himself, watching Lonely play. 'Beats being stuck up here in the hills with just you for company, Jenny La Rue…'

Spoon in hand, he turned to give the weasel a lick of his beans and immediately saw that she was sitting ramrod straight, staring at the front door, ears pricked. In a move that belied his age, Toothless dropped the spoon and strode across the room. Motioning Lonely to be quiet, he reached behind the counter and picked up his shotgun.

Lonely joined him at the window, peering out into the mist and rain. In the background the Moonshiners were still stomping and singing.

'What is it?' whispered Lonely.

'Ain't nobody comes up here in this weather unless they be stupid or sneaky,' Toothless whispered back. 'And I'm guessing whoever it is out there is of the latter persuasion!' He cocked his gun.

Lonely could see nothing but white snowdrifts and slanting rain. Then all of a sudden, out of the corner of his eye, he noticed a snow-covered branch shimmering at the bend in the road, where the pines hung low. It was a Tom camouflaged against the snow in a white overcoat, though the rifle he carried was as black as original sin.

Toothless had already seen him.

'There's a truck full of them back a-ways beyond the bend,' he said grimly. 'And I don't think they're coming to buy postcards.'

Lonely's eyes flared, he felt blood rush to his head.

'You got another shotgun?' he asked, eyes fixed on the Toms outside.

Toothless looked at the Houndling in alarm – this was a side of the little fella that he hadn't seen before. He shook his head and waved Lonely away from the window.

'Even if I did it'd be no use. Them Toms outnumber us ten to one. We gotta get out the back afore they surround the place.'

He grabbed coats and hats, stuffed a box of shotgun shells in one pocket and Jenny La Rue in the other and pushed Lonely towards the back door.

'Grab that guitar of yours, little fella. We won't give them moggrel Toms the pleasure of burning everything worth anything!'

'Burning everything?' Lonely cried as he was bundled out the door.

Toothless cast a last look at his old home.

'When they find the place deserted, them Toms will burn my shack to the ground. It's what they do.'

Lonely felt sick to his stomach. The old Hound was pushing him down a snow-covered trail that led past derelict engines rotting in the yard and through a stand of snowy Firttle Firs to a dark hole in the rock face. Without explanation, Toothless motioned for Lonely to enter.

When his eyes adjusted to the gloom, he realized they were in a dis-used mineshaft. Old timber beams sagged beneath the weight of black rock. An ancient coal cart lay wet and glistening by a pair of rickety rails.

Suddenly there was an explosion outside, followed by a savage, crackling roar. The Toms had torched the store. Grim faced, Tooth-less clambered into the coal cart. He beckoned Lonely to climb in next to a small black keg, which Lonely assumed was full of Houndhooch. Toothless released a rusty lever and the cart squealed as it began to roll forward, slowly at first, then picking up speed. Lonely had no idea where they were going.

'Can the Toms follow us down here?' he cried over the rusty rattle.

Toothless just laughed, picked up the black keg and hurled it towards the entrance. Then, with familiar ease, he swung his double-barrels up and fired both rounds simultaneously. The keg exploded in a roar that shook the beams and every bone in Lonely's body.

The mine entrance had vanished in an avalanche of stone and rubble.

'That sure is powerful Houndhooch!' Lonely said, impressed.

'Houndhooch? That there's *gunpowder*!' hooted Toothless as he turned to navigate the rickety rails.

'Where does this take us?' shouted Lonely, ducking his head as the mineshaft narrowed and the cart rumbled on.

'All the way to freedom!' Toothless shouted back. 'As long as these here rails ain't rotted through!'

⟡

Freedom, it turned out, was not an abstract; it was a place. Freedom Swamp.

Emerging from the tunnel into bright winter sunshine, the coal cart rattled to a halt. Lonely blinked and looked around. They had arrived in a small hamlet in a deep ravine, where ancient Dreary-Willows hung with beardy-moss hemmed a turgid swamp. He could see smoky shacks between the trees, and Hounds in rocking chairs watching them with wary interest from their porches.

'Don't pay them no mind,' said Toothless, flexing his back with an alarming click of vertebrae. 'They're all Juke Moonshiners in this valley. They don't take kindly to strangers. But I knows them well enough: my granddaddy was a Moonshiner and his mama afore that.' He smiled a sad smile. 'Besides, now that I'm officially homeless, I guess I'll be gettin' acquainted with these folks for quite a whiles.'

The Moonshiners were wary of Lonely, and his strange guitar. They took him to a grey timber shack to meet their leader, Elder Spittle, a tall, thin rake of a Hound with stained overalls and eyes the colour of swamp water. He appraised Lonely suspiciously, wrinkling his snout as if at a Cat-carcass. But once Toothless had told them – to Lonely's rising consternation – that the young Hound was an escaped 'gunslinger' who had 'shot that vermin-puss Ruddegan himself' and fled 'an army of mercenary Toms' to be with his 'blood-brother Jukes', they warmed to him some.

Lonely warmed too. As he sat by the crackling fire eating the chilli gumbo served by Elder Spittle's wife, the Hounds of Freedom Swamp began to assemble around him. Soon the timber shack resounded with their laughter, and little Hounds, barefoot and ragged, giggled at the strange 'gun-slinging' Hound smiling to himself by the hearth. The smell of wonderful food permeated the crowded room – swamp-chicken steam-pot, pickled Dreary-Willow pancakes, pepper-eel stew – and the Houndhooch was passed round.

Houndhooch!

Freedom Swamp was renowned in all of Jukedom as the Houndhooch capital of the Shipwoods. In copper stills as old as the hills themselves they brewed and fermented their famous golden tipple, Swamp Fever Tonic.

To the uninitiated it was a taste like no other, but Lonely wrinkled his snout at the first whiff of the firewater and could not bring himself to try it. Toothless, however, was a Houndhooch aficionado. He knew just how to savour the delicious sensations: the burn as it flowed over the tongue, the sudden, alarming, numbing pain, the red-hot poker tickling the tonsils, then the sweetness as if you'd swallowed a beehive, the warm glow deep in your belly.

Summer's End

Lonely had never felt so relaxed, so at home, in all his life. He could not imagine being any happier – until the table was cleared and Elder Spittle announced to the glowing crowd: 'Time to kick a little dust off our boots!'

Suddenly instruments began to appear from all over: ancient guitars, thirteen-string banjos, skiffle boards and harmonicas in all shapes and sizes. Even the smallest Houndlings scrambled to the kitchen and came back with pots and pans to beat.

Elder Spittle's wife stood centre-stage by the fire, and spoke softly to Lonely.

'You are welcome in our home and in our hearts, Lonely Dog. Our brother Toothless Bob tells us that you are quite the musician, so we would be honoured if you'd show us what that kitty-guitar of yours sounds like. Will you lead us in a song?'

Lonely took up his guitar. He had never played his songs to a group before, but now he felt something well up within him – something more than heartburn from the pepper-eel brog. Suddenly he *wanted* to share his songs, wanted to sing for these humble Hounds who had taken him in.

To his surprise he found himself on his feet.

'Good evening, my name is Lonely Dog…' – there was much encouraging stomping and clapping – '…and I'd like to sing you a song that I wrote about my good friend, Toothless Bob.'

Toothless looked startled. Lonely coughed, tweaked the tuning pegs and then, in a voice the Hounds of Freedom Swamp remember to this day, he sang.

> I took a long, long journey
> I was lonely as a dog could be
> I was bleedin' and I was hurtin'
> I'd been travelling with misery
> I tumbled into Blizzard Valley
> I guess I'd travelled miles
> But my pain disappeared like a daydream
> When old Toothless Bob smiled
> When old Toothless Bob smiled
> When old Toothless Bob smiled

When he finished, a hush fell but for the crackle of the logs on the fire. Then, like a cork released from a vintage bottle of Swamp Fever, the room erupted into table-thumping, floor-pounding applause. Old Toothless had tears in his eyes and Elder Spittle was dancing his rake-thin self all over the floor.

They sang on and on into the night, until the envious moon dipped low enough to listen, casting a joyous silver sparkle over Freedom Swamp that made the Dreary-Willows look like Christmas trees.

CHAPTER XVII

Tar-Black Coffee, Swamp Fever Tonic and Pepper-Eel Stew

He's got a Bible in his saddlebag,
And whisky on his tongue
He's got faith to move a mountain
But just in case, he's got a gun.
Some folk say he's the Devil
Some folk claim he's divine
He keeps comin' back like the resurrection
Preaching faith and Moonshine!
Faith and Moonshine!

—Lonely Dog, 'Faith and Moonshine',
from *Gimme That Coal-Time Religion!*

$\mathcal{T}$ime, as is its habit, passed. Almost without noticing,
Lonely realized he had been in Freedom Swamp for over
two years, and had no real plans to move on. He could have,
would have, stayed with the good folk of the Swamp for ever.
Here he had found that rarest and most wonderful thing:
a family. All his life, it seemed to Lonely, he had been on
the outside looking through a grimy window at happiness;
here, in Freedom Swamp, he was finally on the inside.

The Hounds of Freedom Swamp did not have much of anything, in
fact they had equal portions of nothing, but what they had they gladly
shared with him. By day Lonely helped out in the mysterious bubbling
art of Moonshining – though he still could not bring himself to taste the
heady brew. By night he would sing by their fires or listen to all manner
of Juke music on the crackling mountain radio in Elder Spittle's home:
Hill-Billy, Moonshine Skiffle, Heavy Coal-Miners Blues.

In spite of his promise to his nephew, Bronson, Toothless Bob never

did take Lonely on to Molars Post, having become settled himself –
largely due to the ample supply of Houndhooch and the attentions of a
widow Hound named Verna.

In his free time, Lonely would wander the wild mountain trails and
watch the snow melt, the clouds roil, the incandescent sunsets light
the distant peaks. He had never felt so alive. Guitar in hand, he would
sit among the warm tussock grass and play the songs that flooded his
mind.

And think of those he'd left behind.

But as the days grew long and the winter shadows receded, so too did
the faces of his old friends.

Then, one spring morning, when the Dreary-Willows were alive with
swamp-crickets, two pieces of news reached him. They arrived on horseback, brought by none other than Brother Jeroboam himself.

Every second spring the old firebrand saddled his stallion, Righteous,
stuffed his bags with fiery tracts and liquor, and ventured forth from
Molars Post to rouse backsliders in far-flung hamlets, preach against the
vermin-puss and, most of all, to sample the new-vintage Houndhooch.
The last call on his mission was always the most isolated hamlet in his
rocky diocese: Freedom Swamp. And so, on this spring day, when even
the stagnant swamp sparkled with hope, Brother Jeroboam galloped
down the stony trail and into the valley.

The first thing he heard was the sound of a strange guitar, lighter
and sharper than the heavy-stringed Juke guitars back at Molars, with a
twang that reminded him of … a Cat fiddle? He cantered Righteous to a
stop and swung his six-foot frame round in the saddle to see where it was

coming from. Leaning against a tree trunk, feet dangling in the shimmering swamp water, sat Lonely, eyes closed, picking out a tune. Brother Jeroboam trotted over.

'You, my young friend,' he intoned with a voice like gravel thrown over corrugated iron, 'must be the famous renegade, Lonely Dog.'

Lonely's eyes flew open. Seeing the imposing, moustached Hound astride the horse, he leapt to his feet in fear.

'How d'you know my name, sir?' he managed to say. 'And why do you call me a "famous renegade"? I ain't either of those.'

Brother Jeroboam swung out of the saddle, took a red bandana from his pocket, dipped it in the water and wiped his hot brow.

'That's not what I hear on the mountain radio,' he said, turning to stare at the small Hound. Lonely was reminded of the first time he was called to Headmaster Flannegan's office, shaking like a leaf.

'On the radio? I don't understand, sir. I've never been on the radio…'

'A *modest* renegade!' The preacher laughed heartily. 'Well, at least admit to being Lonely Dog.'

Perplexed, Lonely again asked the stranger how he knew his name.

'The fact that you begin every performance with the words "Good evening, I'm Lonely Dog" is a bit of a giveaway!' Brother Jeroboam guffawed out loud, throwing his big head back at his own wry joke.

Suddenly it dawned on Lonely what the old Hound was talking about. Elder Spittle, like many mountain Hounds, was an avid radio ham. He must have recorded Lonely's nightly fireside performances and broadcast them on his radio out across the Shipwoods and Juke hamlets. Clearly Toothless Bob had added his two-pennies' worth with his tales of the 'renegade Hound gunslinger from Alveridge'. Lonely wished the ground would open up and swallow him.

Sensing his embarrassment, Brother Jeroboam laid a grizzled hand on the young Hound's shoulder. 'You didn't realize you were being broadcast, did you?'

Lonely shook his head.

'Well, you've got nothing to be ashamed of, young Lonely Dog! Your songs have become the stuff of legend in these parts – even if you do play them on that moggrel contraption you call a guitar. My own wife wants me to have them sung in the Cathedral back in Molars Post!'

Lonely looked up, startled, recognition flooding his face.

'You must be Brother Jeroboam. I've heard you on the radio!'

'One and the same!' He smiled. 'Looks like we both got ourselves famous!'

∿

That night, after a dinner at Elder Spittle's home in Brother Jeroboam's honour, the old preacher drew Lonely aside. They sat on the porch, Lonely on the stoop and Brother Jeroboam on a creaking rocking chair, packing a baccy-pipe. A goose-owl hooted in the Dreary-Willows. From indoors came the sound of instruments tuning up.

'These folk are like kin to you, ain't they?' he asked, his voice so low Lonely had to strain forward to hear.

'They *are* my family,' he replied emphatically.

Brother Jeroboam lit his pipe and blew a smoke ring into the night.

'What about your *other* family?' he said quietly.

Lonely looked at him uncertainly. 'Who do you mean?'

'The family you left behind back in Port Alveridge.'

The old Hound did not look at him but the words struck Lonely in the pit of his stomach. He thought of Port Alveridge less and less often now, and when he did what he mostly felt was guilt.

'I think about them as often as I can,' was all he managed to say.

Brother Jeroboam stopped puffing on his pipe and turned to Lonely. The porch light made his winged moustache glow.

'There is a time to think, and there is a time to act. I have ridden over the mountains to Freedom Swamp to bring you this message, Lonely: the time to act is now upon you!'

Towards Port Alveridge

'I don't understand…' Lonely's face was a map of confusion. 'You rode all this way to tell me to act? *To act upon what?*'

Brother Jeroboam rose to his full, commanding height, stared out towards the swamp alive with chirping-frogs, then up into the star-flecked sky; finally he looked back to Lonely seated at his feet.

'At this very moment, Bronson, whom you call your brother, is holed up in Ruddegan's prison at Fever Creek. His crime? Being free! The Felines are positioning for absolute power. Many Hounds are moving out of Port Alveridge. Even worse, the only voice we Hounds have left is the Baron's. He's the only one with the courage to make a stand no matter what. His voice, unfortunately, few understand, as he speaks in the riddles and rantings of an old Hound. Many Hounds are heading into the surrounding hinterlands, giving up, never to return. They are strangers in their own land. These are hard times, Lonely. The Felines seek to scatter us and take over our land. The Hounds of Alveridgea need a voice, and you, my modest little renegade, might just be that voice. Your songs remind us who we really are. It's time for us to broadcast this message to all the Hounds across Greater Alveridgea!'

CHAPTER XVIII

The Cat-Shaped Key and the Instrumentorium

Kick down the door!!
Smash a few chairs!!
Break a few bottles!!
Does anybody care!?
We gonna kick the sun to Sunday!!
We gonna break the break of dawn!!
We ain't going quietly!
They'll have to take us with guns drawn!!

— Goth Guzzle and the Knuckledusters,
from *Shipwood Mountain Wedding Songs*

*M*olars Post, situated at the highest point in the Shipwoods, had been founded by Brother Jeroboam's great-grandfather, Vinegar Joesephus, who had personally overseen every aspect of its construction. The town had been hewn out of the granite mountainside and now, generations later, was almost as grey and bleak, as cold and windswept, as the stone itself.

These were Lonely's thoughts as he sat behind Brother Jeroboam on his stallion, Righteous, clopping along the town's cobblestone streets. It was one week to the day since Lonely had bid farewell to his friends at Freedom Swamp and set out with Brother Jeroboam.

It had taken some persuasion for him to leave the valley of tumbling shacks nestled between the Dreary-Willows and Houndhooch stills twinkling in the sun. But Brother Jeroboam's news of Bronson's plight had fired a restlessness already stirring within him, a yearning like the twanging of a bass string deep in his heart.

Lonely was ready to venture further down the strange highway of life.

'You have a rare gift, my small friend,' Brother Jeroboam had told him, 'the gift of weaving words and tunes to wrap around a Hound's very soul. Your music moves us, Lonely, and that is a wonderful and a dangerous gift indeed.'

Now, as they rode into Molars Post, Lonely wondered what those dangers might be. He shivered, despite the spring sunshine, as Righteous trotted past storefronts full of engine parts, a haberdashery where most items were made of the same grey denim, and a barber's shop where old bearded Hounds sat smoking silently on wooden benches. Everything was caked in coal-dust and grit and the streets were deserted.

'The men-folk are down the mines and the lady-folk are schooling the Houndlings in their homes,' Brother Jeroboam said, as though reading Lonely's thoughts. 'Tonight will be very different. Place comes to life after dark.'

He tethered Righteous to a rusty railing outside a huge building in the centre of town. Lonely gazed up at the two square pillars that supported a stone portico emblazoned with the words: 'Heavy Toil and Heavy Music'. Fearsome gargoyle Hound-heads with flowing granite beards and pious stony stares glowered down at him.

'Welcome to my Cathedral of Rock!' boomed the preacher, stepping inside.

Lonely scurried after him into a place such as he had never seen, so vast, so vaulted and so… empty. The floor was laid with flagstones, the walls were solid stone stained green with age, there were no windows, no pews, nothing but a massive stone platform and, behind it, a great black curtain. The only light came from a giant chandelier made of hundreds of miners' lanterns welded to a huge steel wheel.

'Tonight this sacred place will reverberate with true and undefiled Hound Sound!' Brother Jeroboam declared, arms raised, eyes shining like wet coal. 'But first, bring that kitty-guitar of yours and follow me to the Instrumentorium.'

The preacher led the way down a winding flight of hidden stairs to a door of heavy ironwood. From his breast pocket he removed a key shaped like a dead Cat and fitted it into the lock. The Instrumentorium was a vast cellar of low-slung beams and stone, but it did not store Houndhooch or sacks of coal. It stored guitars. In rows that stretched as far as the eye could see, serried ranks of guitars stood straight as a regiment of the Baron's Houndsford Fusiliers, glowing in the flickering light of hundreds of candles set in wrought-iron stands.

There were guitars the like of which Lonely had never come across before – stringed and fretted like Alveridgean and Trumaine guitars but shaped and styled in copper and bronze, with steel heads and necks and strange chrome plates. Each had a panel of knobs and switches like the dashboard of a pick-up truck, and from each dangled a coil of wire and a bulbous black plug.

'Go ahead, try one, Lonely!' Brother Jeroboam cried.

Lonely stopped by a huge steel Thrummer shaped like a comet's tail, covered in a patina of rust. He slipped it over his shoulder, feeling its weight cut into his flesh, and strummed a chord. The sound that emerged was tinny and weak and Lonely glanced at the preacher, bewildered.

'It don't sound like it looks,' he said.

'Oh, it will tonight, my friend!' laughed Brother Jeroboam. 'Once we get it amped!'

'Amped?'

'Sure! They all need *amplification!*' From the preacher's lips the word sounded like 'redemption' or 'salvation'. 'Come, let me show you the workshop.'

Lonely replaced the guitar and followed.

In the workshop a large Juke Hound with a braided white beard and copper-rimmed spectacles was seated at a cluttered workbench covered with a mystifying array of tools and contraptions. There were ratchets and valves and dozens of things Lonely did not recognize; they all trailed copper wire, and some ticked and hummed and buzzed alarmingly.

'This here is Brother Luther.'

'Did you make all those things in the Instrumentorium?' Lonely asked. Peering at what Brother Luther was doing, he almost got his snout singed in a jet of blue flame as the old Hound welded a spot on the guitar he had in front of him.

'Made 'em, tweaked 'em, fixed 'em, each and every one.' Luther's eyes shone behind his glasses. 'Been making and tweaking and fixing since I were a Houndling. Engines it were back then; I worked the ships that plied the Esparrow Sea. Started out scrubbing decks, but my heart was always in the engine room.'

'Why?' said Lonely, bewildered.

'Not rightly sure I know. Something about the power of the pistons and the steam… The clanging and hissing was like Houndskiffle to me. Danced me a jig the day they put me in charge of the twin-cylinder double-walking beam engine on old *Miss Liberty* – back when she was doing the russock run. I had her purring like a Kitterling – 'scuse my language – there was nothing ol' *Liberty* wouldn't do for me. It was in the engine room I got to making instruments. Me, a stoker and a couple of stevedores had the first Pneumatic Blues Quartet in Alveridgea.' Brother Luther paused and stared away for a thoughtful moment. 'To think that she is now a prison ship for Hounds…'

'And then,' Brother Jeroboam boomed, 'he saw the light. Day they retired *Miss Liberty,* I persuaded him to come to the mountains, to work with me and my flock. Without Brother Luther here there would be no Hound Sound. There ain't nothing stringed or dinged he can't fix – he'll get that Cat fiddle of yours fixed and ready…'

'Fixed?' Lonely looked even more confused.

'Amped!' cried Brother Jeroboam. 'Amped and ready! 'Cause if you step up to play in my Cathedral with that kitty-guitar like it is, it's going to sound like a Cat fiddle in a force-nine gale. You need to be able to crank up the volume, my son, so you leave your instrument with our guitar surgeon, Doctor Luther, and come along with me.'

'Where we going now?' Lonely asked, not sure he wanted to leave his precious guitar with 'Doctor' Luther.

'You'll see the Doctor again soon enough. Right now we've got some planning to do if we want to get your message across all of Alveridgea.'

CHAPTER XIX

The Sanctuary of Rock

And verily after they have toiled mightily
They shall enter the Sanctuary of Rock,
And thus they shall stompeth and clappeth
    and loudly proclaim
With amplified music and the wailing of many guitars
    The Faith which is their Houndly inheritance.
    And no Cat shall hinder them nor bid them be silent,
    For such is an abomination in these
        Sacred Mountains.

—*The Second Book of Juke*, Chapter xxxv, v. 678

*F*rom its headwaters high in the Shipwood Mountains
flows a stream called Sanctuary Creek. It begins as a
trickle but quickly gains momentum, drawing other
streams into a surging river whose mighty whitewater
thunders over waterfalls then winds through Molars
Post and ends its journey at Vinegar Lake.

Lonely had crossed Sanctuary Creek on horseback that day with Brother
Jeroboam; they had followed its course from the mountains above Freedom Swamp all the way to Molars Post. Now, as he stood on the steps
of the Cathedral of Rock, with the moon nailed to a coal-black sky,
Lonely watched another river forming – a river of Juke Hounds! They
trickled from their grey-stone houses, merged and flowed into a swell
that streamed inexorably towards the Cathedral, flooded through the
huge doorway and pooled into a mighty lake of Jukes within the echoing sanctuary. There, waiting for them, arms raised and illuminated by
a hidden spotlight, was Brother Jeroboam. He stood astride the granite

platform, like a great bearded prophet shrouded in a large brown cape, staff in hand.

Lonely had never seen so many Hounds united in single-minded purpose. Young and old, bearded and braided, male and female stood shoulder to shoulder, a sea of upturned snouts, lit by the flickering glow of the hundred lanterns that dangled above them.

They wore nothing fancy, just the grey denim overalls of their every-day workwear, still caked with coal-dust and oil smears. Lonely, who had neatly pressed his old black suit and dusted off his white shirt and tie, felt ridiculously overdressed.

The Cathedral doors clanged shut, the great assembly fell silent,

Juke Hounds

'Brother and Sister Jukes!' he thundered in a voice that would raise the dead and make them dance. 'Have you toiled by the sweat of your brow this day?'

'We have so toiled!' came the deafening reply.

'And have you, by this hard toil, purged yourselves of wanton idleness?' the preacher boomed.

'We have so purged our very souls!'

'And therefore, by the sweat of your brow that cleanses your soul, and by the renunciation of all that is Feline and fornicated, are you ready to receive the Sacred Benediction?'

'We are ready indeed!'

There came the thunderous thump of a thousand hounds dropping to one knee. Lonely quickly followed suit.

'In accordance with your penitent spirits, and by the bending of your knees, I proclaim you purged and pardoned and partakers of the Hallowed Faith of our Houndly Forefathers! Arise my Brethren and let these mountains shake with the one, true *Sound of the Hound*!'

With a flourish, he pulled on a cord. The massive black curtains parted to reveal the magnificent steam-powered Juke Box.

Lonely stared in stunned silence as all around him the Jukes erupted into stomping, chanting, cheering.

Brother Jeroboam hushed them with his outstretched hands.

'Now is the time I would normally release a disc on the sacred Juke Box, that we might mosh together. But not tonight!'

A ripple of consternation ran through the congregation, with much shaking of braided beards.

'Hear me, Brethren!' Brother Jeroboam cried. 'I understand your confusion! But tonight, for your edification and enlightenment, I have brought one even more glorious for you to listen to! Let us welcome him to our stage!'

Caught up in the expectant spirit of the evening, Lonely clapped and stomped, glancing round to see who the mysterious performer could be. Then the spotlight swung away from Brother Jeroboam and picked out the little hound's startled face.

'Brethren, you have heard him on the radio, sung his songs as you have toiled. All the way from Freedom Swamp, the little minstrel with the big voice… LONELY DOG! Make way for our small brother!'

Suddenly the sea of Juke Hounds parted and a path appeared, washed in light, all the way to the stage. Stunned, caught in the glare of the spotlight, Lonely could neither move nor make a sound. Tentatively he took a single step, as though off the edge of a cliff. Then, his heart pounding, his head spinning, he took another, and another and before he knew it he found himself next to Brother Jeroboam, standing beside the great Juke Box.

At his feet a thousand faces beamed.

'But I haven't got my guitar…' was all he could mumble.

Brother Jeroboam smiled and beckoned to a figure at the side of the stage. Brother Luther came striding across, light dancing off his copper-rimmed glasses, carrying something in a black cloth. He handed it to Lonely, saying, 'I had to make a few adjustments, but I think you'll find she sounds like a five-string avalanche.'

Lonely removed the black cloth and stared in wonderment at the guitar he'd built from kitty-fiddles in the Catside shed all those years ago. Brother Luther had worked his magic and the battered instrument now boasted six metal plates between the fretboard and the bridge, five strange knobs that sprouted like mushrooms along the bottom edge, and a coil of wire. The strings had been replaced with industrial wire, as had the wooden tuning pegs, which were now bronze machine heads, each shaped like a braying Hound.

Lonely strummed the new strings uncertainly and found he produced the same lifeless sound he'd made on the Thrummer in the Instrumentorium, lost as wind in a telegraph wire. He turned to Brother Jeroboam, hoping he might be able to just slip back into the crowd, but the preacher stopped him.

'It sounds like Granny's clothesline!' the preacher laughed. 'But that's because you ain't been amped.' Then he pointed to the great Juke Box behind him and cried, 'Amp him, Brother Luther, and amp him good!'

Brother Luther sprang forward, grabbed the wire that trailed from Lonely's guitar and plugged it into a socket in the Juke Box. There was a hush of expectation in the vast crowd, and all was silent apart from the rattle of a coal truck emptying its last load into the giant hopper outside. As if on cue, Luther yanked an oily lever and the steam-powered engine roared into life, throbbing like a team of wagon horses waiting for the command to gallop.

'What do I do now?' Lonely asked anxiously as his guitar began to vibrate in his hands.

By way of an answer Brother Luther unravelled a wired contraption attached to a long chrome pole and angled it inches from Lonely's startled snout. 'That there's a microphone,' was all he said.

Lonely stared down at the fervent faces, cast a nervous look at Brother Jeroboam, who nodded in encouragement. But Lonely's brain, like a needle at the end of a record, skipped and repeated.

'I can't do this! There are too many Hounds...' he whispered.

Brother Jeroboam laid a gentle hand on the small Hound's shoulder.

'Just pretend you're back at Elder Spittle's fireside and the Hounds of Freedom Swamp have gathered at the end of a hard day's toil. Close your eyes, imagine... *and sing!*'

Lonely closed his eyes. He saw Toothless Bob smiling at him with Verna in his embrace, saw Elder Spittle and his wife, and all the Hounds he called his family, poor as dirt but rich of spirit, gathered round the crackling fire. And behind them, he saw other shadowy faces: Big Bronson, arms folded, winking at him; Bella, hands clasped, proud as punch; old Rolph, tapping time; and Kelzie, her eyes shimmering in soft light, whispering across the years: 'Sing, Lonely, sing!'

He opened his eyes, stepped forward to the strange microphone and said, 'Good evening, my name is Lonely Dog!'

The roar of the congregation was lost in the roar of Lonely's first chord, which thundered through the Cathedral like a

Lonely Dog Sings

thousand stampeding cattle. The Juke Hounds stood their ground, ears pinned back by the deafening volume, eyes squeezed tight in excitement. Brother Jeroboam himself was all but blown from the stage.

And then, in a voice that hit the crowd like a sledgehammer, Lonely began to sing.

> I was hurting, and bleeding, and needing redeeming
> I was burning, and yearning, on a road with no turning
> I was searching for Freedom Road
>
> Freedom Road got a lot of dead ends
> Freedom Road ain't on no map
> But I know that long road to Freedom
> Begins when there's no turning back
>
> I was lost but I got found, I was homeless yet homeward bound
> Every door was locked, but opened when I knocked
> I was walking down Freedom Road
>
> Freedom Road got a lot of dead ends
> Freedom Road ain't on no map
> But I know that long road to Freedom
> Begins when there's no turning back
>
> Freedom Road is free, but the price is steep
> Freedom Road is free, but it don't come cheap
> Freed of my load on Freedom Road

Freedom Road got a lot of dead ends

Freedom Road ain't on no map

But I know that long road to Freedom

Begins when there's no turning back

Back in Beaconsfield, the Baron kept close watch on the array of dials as his pirate station beamed the message all the way to Felinea and right across Greater Alveridgea.

A. K. Ruddegan rose to his feet, quivering with rage, and savagely switched off the radio.

'This must stop!' he snarled at Warden O'Grady sitting stiffly at the end of the long boardroom table. 'If I only knew where I could get my hands on that lawless mongrel, I would dispose of him once and for all!'

O'Grady was a huge Cat of middle years, squeezed into a tight grey suit. His belly spilled over his belt in a landslide of sweaty flesh and the collar of his standard-issue white shirt was unbuttoned to compensate for his many chins; though he wore a regulation black tie, it hung like a hangman's noose. His ginger hair was cropped indecently short in the manner of bureau-Cats, his grey eyes were chillingly void of warmth. At first glance he looked like a bully, but he had long since stopped bullying. Now he was a sadist in a cheap suit.

Warden O'Grady looked thoughtful, then sat up straight, stubbing out his cigarette. With a distant gaze towards the hinterlands he quietly spoke.

'I know where he is. I know where Lonely Dog is hiding.'

He spun round, revelation all over his face. A. K. looked on and waited, all ears.

'You heard it too – at the beginning of the broadcast. The Baron introduced him, then said "Going live to a secret location". In that pause before he started playing… didn't you hear it? The faint sound of a coal truck in the background. I knew I recognized the sound of that weird clanking hoist. It delivers our coal to the prison ship, *Miss Liberty*. What's-his-name Four Trucks was delivering coal right beside wherever Lonely Dog is! Four Trucks gets his coal from some coal-mining town up in the Shipwoods. We can find him!'

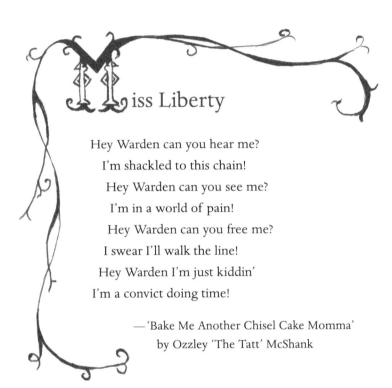

CHAPTER XX

Miss Liberty

Hey Warden can you hear me?
I'm shackled to this chain!
Hey Warden can you see me?
I'm in a world of pain!
Hey Warden can you free me?
I swear I'll walk the line!
Hey Warden I'm just kiddin'
I'm a convict doing time!

— 'Bake Me Another Chisel Cake Momma'
by Ozzley 'The Tatt' McShank

*T*here was a time when heads would turn
at the graceful curves and long, seductive lines of
Miss Liberty. A time when folks would stop and stare
at such a fine-looking steamship belle. But no more.

Now she was a rust-bucket, chained to the jetty like a mongrel cur, stained with fifty years of hard living and abuse, her sinuous contours broken by watchtowers, her huge black smokestacks the only reminder of her former life as a cargo ship plying the Esparrow Sea. Now she was a rotting prison hulk moored to peeling pylons in a malarial backwater of Fever Creek. Her portholes were barred, her cabins filthy cells, her intricate wrought-iron railings replaced with razor wire. Inside, five hundred convict Hounds sweated in the broiling heat and froze when the cruel winter winds blew. Plagued by black clouds of swamp-mosquitoes and the stench of sewage seeping from blocked pipes, they watched the world slip by like flotsam on the tidal wash.

This was what Hounds meant by 'Upriver'.

The prison ship, like so many municipally funded projects, was controlled by Mayor Ruddegan, who insisted – in an uncustomary flare of irony – that the crumbling hulk retain the name *Miss Liberty*. Over cigars and cognac at his private club he liked to joke with his Fat Cat associates that, far from being locked up, the convicted Hounds were actually living 'in *Liberty*'!

Now, however, as his black Pussington limousine shuddered to a halt at the Fever Creek jetty, Mayor Ruddegan was not laughing. He detested the journey 'Upriver' – the rutted tracks and dismal swampland, the derelict hamlets of rickety shacks with their barefoot Houndlings and glowering parents, the muggy heat that made his white silk suit stick to his back. And today he had more reason than usual to feel toxic.

A small bump behind his left ear throbbed painfully. It had been over two years since the fateful night his granddaughter had assaulted him and, though there had been no long-term effects, at certain times the swelling would return and pulsate as insistently as the hellish Houndskiffle she had liked to listen to. Of course Celia had not really been at fault. She had acted in the heat of the moment, clearly under the pernicious influence of that grotesque Houndling, Lonely Dog. *He* was to blame, with his lecherous Hound music; *he* had trespassed on Ruddegan's property and had no doubt wanted to entice his granddaughter away.

The throbbing behind Ruddegan's well-coiffed ear reminded him that the little cur was still a free Hound. But not for much longer, hopefully. The Mayor had done his utmost to blacken Lonely Dog's name. He'd informed the Port Alveridge police and the Powers in Felinea that Lonely was a member of the Hound Resistance sent to assassinate him and kidnap his granddaughter. The incident had been part of an evil Hound conspiracy, he'd assured the authorities. No one had doubted the Mayor's word, especially as Ruddegan had offered a substantial reward for Lonely Dog's head.

To ensure that no one could contradict his version of events, Ruddegan had despatched his granddaughter to St Bilius Convent, where all Felines took vows of silence and lived in small cell-like rooms. It irked him that their vows of silence were not matched by vows of poverty – keeping Celia under lock and key was costing him a small fortune. But once Celia was incommunicado, the search for Lonely Dog had begun in earnest.

The Powers in Felinea duly despatched a convoy of enforcers to search for the would-be assassin. They traced him to a fuel station in Blizzard

Blue Dress

Valley on the edge of the Shipwoods, but the cunning Hound eluded them and disappeared into Juke territory. In the two years since, nothing had been heard of Lonely Dog and Ruddegan had begun to think that he'd seen the last of the little cur. But recently he had resurfaced, bolder than ever, a nascent hero to Hounds everywhere, performing every night on the radio.

Port Blues, the Hounds' local radio station in Port Alveridge, had broadcast for as long as anyone could remember, playing a steady mix of Houndskiffle and Working-Hound Blues, funded by harmless commercials for tow-trucks and plumbing supplies. But recently the Hounds of Port Alveridge had been tuning into a different frequency – Beaconsfield Live. This pirate radio station was broadcast by powerful transmitters from the Baron's castle in Beaconsfield. Until now, the Hounds had shown no interest in the isolationist rantings of a defiant old war veteran: Port Hounds had always preferred rhythm and blues to rhetoric and politics. But their ears started to prick up when Beaconsfield Radio began to relay the mesmerizing music of an unheard-of Hound with a distinctive guitar style – live – from a secret location. The broadcast, at 8.37 every evening, had been going strong now for months, ever since Lonely had moved to Molars Post. Word of mouth was spreading the message like wildfire and hundreds of new listeners were tuning in every evening.

The slot always began with the words: 'Good evening, my name is Lonely Dog!' The music that followed was a strange fusion of Houndskiffle, Houndhooch-Stomp and startling Cat-inflected jazz, but it was the songs that had so many Hounds tuning in. They spoke of a simple life, of love and loss, of the dignity of work, the joys of family. And they spoke of protest – for equality, for fair pay, for workers' rights. Above all, the songs of Lonely Dog talked of harmony: between father and son, mother and daughter, boss and worker, rich and poor.

He even went so far as to sing of harmony between Hound and Cat.

It was this that got Mayor Ruddegan's blood boiling. He began to receive troubling late-night phone calls from the Generals' Office in Felinea, demanding that action be taken to silence these broadcasts. Accordingly he had sent his Tom enforcers to destroy rebel radio antennas. Their early raids in the foothills below the Shipwoods left a trail of burning villages and toppled transmitters but to venture further into the mountain stronghold of the Jukes would require a much more significant force. It would require an army.

This new thorn in Ruddegan's side diverted him from his old archenemy the Baron of Beaconsfield, who – despite having been subjected to numerous raids and even a frontal assault by armed Toms – was still holed up in his fortified estate, haranguing all and sundry. Even more humiliating than his anti-Feline tirades was that the Baron had personally led a counter attack of musket-firing veterans and seen off a phalanx of heavily armed Toms.

Ruddegan rubbed the bump behind his ear and stared morosely out of his limo window. Things were not going according to plan. If he could not control the Hounds in his own province then the Generals in Felinea would step in and remove him from power. A banging on his window snapped him back to reality. It was his chauffeur, a mirthless Tom – weren't they all – named Cudgell.

'We have arrived, sir.' Cudgell opened the door and the blast of fetid air made Ruddegan choke. 'Warden O'Grady is waiting by the gate.'

Reluctantly the Mayor stepped out into the heat and stench of Fever Creek.

∾

Warden O'Grady was standing by the iron gate at the prison jetty. It was surmounted with razor wire and flanked by ominous watchtowers from which Toms with machine-guns impassively watched the Mayor approach. O'Grady greeted Mayor A. K. Ruddegan with a dead-fish smile and a clammy grip.

'Welcome to Fever Creek, Mr Mayor,' he said in a voice strangled by five packs a day.

'So what's so pressing that it calls me to this stink-hole so urgently?' spat Ruddegan.

With a wry smile, O'Grady paused, then replied quietly, 'We have the dog! My Toms delivered Lonely Dog here just two hours ago. We slammed him in the hold and I called you straight away.'

A. K.'s response was stunned silence. Finally his moment had come. His mind raced with all manner of schemes.

'Does anyone know?' A. K. realized he had no real reason to detain the popular wee Hound.

'Not so far. Just me, and my guys that hauled him in,' O'Grady replied with a smug smirk.

A. K.'s eyes darted from side to side as he processed this exquisite news.

'We can talk in my office,' the Warden said, snapping his fingers at the brawny Toms guarding the gate. 'It'll be cooler there.'

There was a rattle of chains and the gates clanked open. The two Cats walked down the wooden jetty towards *Miss Liberty*, which was leaning drunkenly against the pilings. Black smoke belched from the twin smoke-stacks and hung in the windless air like a contagion.

Warden O'Grady led the way up the metal gangplank and on to the ship. At the top of a circular stairwell they entered the old deck house, now his office. The ship's wheel was still in place, framed by corroded brass levers and dials.

The Warden gestured Ruddegan to a stained leather couch as he slid his own obese frame behind a desk cluttered with files. From a brimming ashtray he fished out a half-smoked cigarette and relit it. The Mayor took a cigar from his breast pocket and did likewise. A rickety fan sliced the air overhead.

'So what now?' the Warden finally asked, desperately interested in the role he might play in whatever happened next.

Ruddegan leaned back on the couch and blew a thick stream of cigar smoke upwards. 'How many inmates have you got on old *Miss Liberty?*' he asked.

Warden O'Grady flipped open a folder and ran a fat finger down a long column of figures.

'As of today… about five hundred, but that doesn't include another transportation arriving tonight of thirteen more Howlers. So, that'll make five hundred and thirteen in total.'

'Sounds a bit… overcrowded,' Ruddegan said with mock concern. 'I mean to say, it can't be sanitary having all those grubby Hounds kennelled up together, now can it?'

The Warden stared at him, uncertain as to where the conversation was headed. 'Well, by *law* we are only supposed to have two hundred inmates here at Fever Creek…' He trailed off, waiting for the Mayor's response.

It came in the form of a sinister laugh.

'The law?' Ruddegan scoffed. '"Upriver", Warden, *you and I* are the law! Don't forget that.' He wiped sweat from his forehead. 'You got something to drink? I could down a river!'

The Warden opened his desk drawer and removed two tumblers and a half-empty bottle. He splashed some into the glasses and the two Cats sat back and sipped for a while, eyeing each other.

'So, what do you suggest I do about my "illegal overcrowding"?' the Warden asked cautiously.

Ruddegan stood, glass in one hand, cigar in the other, and crossed to the window. He pointed to the rusty decks and coils of barbed wire below.

'I'm not suggesting anything, Warden. Far be it for me to tell you how to run your ship. Still, I can't help but feel that, what with all this over-crowding, it's just an accident waiting to happen.' He turned slowly, his black eyes glittering, and held the Warden's gaze.

'"Accident waiting to happen",' O'Grady repeated with a sinister curl of his mouth. 'What kind of "accident" were you thinking of, Mr Mayor?'

Ruddegan resumed his seat and held up the butt of his cigar. He gently blew on the black ash-tip until it glowed fiery red.

'Oh, I don't know. Why, some fool could inadvertently drop a cigar butt in the cell block and before you know it the whole place could be an inferno and those poor old Hounds, all locked up and shackled… Why, they wouldn't stand a chance. Now that would be tragic, wouldn't it, Warden?'

O'Grady gave a smile like a knife slash.

'It could only be more tragic if some fool had accidentally turned off the water to the fire-hoses.'

Ruddegan stubbed his butt in the Warden's ashtray, then ran his fingers over his impeccable whiskers.

'I'm so glad you share my concerns about the hazards of overcrowding. I think we both know that something needs to be done urgently to remedy the situation. Consider it a burning issue.'

Ruddegan turned on his heel and left.

Peering through the barred porthole of his cell, Bronson watched Ruddegan striding down the jetty towards the main gate.

'What's Ruddegan doing up here?' he growled to himself. 'Look at that smug smirk. Give me five minutes with him in this cell and I'd wipe the smile off his face!'

'Can't be done, Bronson.' His cellmate was a broom-thin Howler named Jethro. 'Even if you got Ruddegan in here, there ain't room to swing a Cat!' He collapsed on to his steel cot in laughter.

Bronson didn't laugh, just stared angrily after the Mayor. He'd managed to elude the Toms for more than two years after that night he'd left Lonely Dog with Toothless Bob in Blizzard Valley. Mostly he'd hidden out in Beaconsfield with the Baron. Then, a month ago, he'd gone to meet a little Houndette he was half in love with, Shardona, at Gnarling Point. He was ambushed. Fifty Toms, big and mean, had surrounded him and the ensuing brawl had been spectacular and desperate. Eventually the Toms had got the better of him. They chained and shackled the big Hound, beat him to a bloody pulp, then hauled him off to Fever Creek.

As the armoured van bounced 'Upriver' over rutted roads, the manacles digging into his bloody flesh and his eye swelling like a rotten avocado, Bronson couldn't shake one sickening thought: how had the Toms known he'd be at Gnarling Point? He hadn't told the other Howlers, hadn't told anyone. Only Shardona herself had known he was coming, and Bronson was certain she wouldn't have betrayed him.

The Baron had invited Bronson to dinner that night and, as always, had spent most of the evening reliving past glories and marshalling battalions of salt shakers and cutlery in ferocious battle. Bronson had finally

Inside the Sun Curry House

slipped away, telling the old Hound he had a secret assignation with a pair of hot lips at Gnarling Point. The Baron had generously offered him a bottle of vintage Houndstooth Pinot for the date and wished him well.

It had taken Bronson thirty minutes by bike from Beaconsfield to the Point – time enough for the Toms to prepare an attack if someone had phoned to alert them, someone who knew of his midnight rendezvous. And aside from the old Baron, the only other Hound at the dinner table that evening had been an old friend fallen on hard times. Rolph Flannegan.

Mayor Ruddegan hurried through the heat to his limousine, a river of sweat flowing down the fur on his back. His silk suit would be ruined, and his white patent-leather brogues were already stained with rust.

No matter, he was happy, smug with vindication. His day of vengeance had finally come.

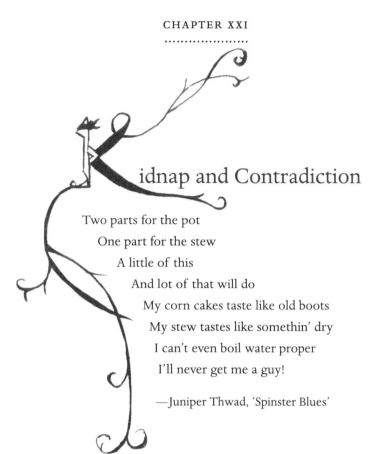

CHAPTER XXI

Kidnap and Contradiction

Two parts for the pot
One part for the stew
A little of this
And lot of that will do
My corn cakes taste like old boots
My stew tastes like somethin' dry
I can't even boil water proper
I'll never get me a guy!

—Juniper Thwad, 'Spinster Blues'

*L*arry Four Trucks slumped on the front porch
alongside Brother Luther. Lonely's disappearance
had shocked Molars Post; the town was in mourning,
and there had been no more nightly broadcasts.

'A. K.'s thugs,' said Luther in disgust. 'Wait till the Baron broadcasts
this!' He gazed morosely down the valley from his rustic rocking chair
and wondered just what had gone wrong. The Toms had come on a
night as dark as ink. Car headlights had been seen casting shadows on
the wide stony bluffs, but it wasn't known how they'd found Lonely. Had
there been a traitor amongst them, a Judas? But why? Why would any
Hound turn on their unlikely hero and betray him?

⌒

Like ripples across a pond, word had spread of Lonely's nightly broadcasts,
and thousands had been tuning in – Hounds from not only Alveridgea,
but also Malconrowe, Trumaine and as far off as Blackenrowe. Even
in the Cat stronghold of Felinea, radios were being covertly tuned and

played low and soft, heads huddled close to hear every forbidden note. No one had any idea where he was. That secret was being well kept.

Lonely was oblivious to all this. He didn't even own a radio, let alone listen to one. He was too focused on scrawling down his latest lyrics on anything he had to hand – old notebooks or the backs of paper bags. He poured out his soul, giving a surprisingly public airing to his normally closely guarded emotions, all in an endeavour to make sense of the con-fusing world in which he found himself. And through Lonely's slightly nervous voice, his growing legions of fans heard their own thoughts and frustrations expressed, as feelings hidden deep came rushing to the surface.

In the communal dining hall Lonely had met a group of minstrels known as the Sunshine Boys. These guys were good. They'd never set foot in a coal mine and, judging from the way they dressed, were clearly not intending to. They played for their keep as the resident Molars Post band.

Mick was the leader. A black-and-white Trumainian, taller than most, he wore his ears tied back and favoured dark-rimmed spectacles, a long green coat, and platform shoes that made him seem even taller. Mick played three-string bass, or the Twangler, as it was known. Trumainians made the finest three-strings, and Mick was all over the fretboard, like a grasshopper on a dance floor. Leroy Chandelier was an odd one. He dressed similar to Mick, looked like a long-eared ringmaster in a blue coat, and played a mean Howlerphone. Little Buddy played honky-tonk keys – 'tickler of the ivories' is how he put it. Hammer, the drummer, introduced himself as 'the skin beater', slapped his belly like a drum roll and then roared with laughter as he shook Lonely's hand.

The Sunshine Boys had a place in the dining room with their gear permanently installed for nightly gigs. It was here, while all the town was out working the mines, that Lonely would sometimes join them for rehearsals. The cooks would look on in wonder at the sensation they had become. Increasingly they began to be Lonely's backing band on his broadcasts.

The sparsely furnished lodgings Uncle Jeroboam had arranged for Lonely was typical of most miners' places at Molars Post. It stood at the end of Sawpit Row, a lane with dozens of identical weatherboard shacks, rusty roofs and crooked tin chimneys standing side by side. Verandas were cluttered with clothes lines draped with overalls and diapers, and with old sofas, car parts and bulging sacks of coal. Lonely's room was simple, furnished with a coal stove for warmth, a chair, a washbasin and a single electric light bulb with switch-cord hanging from the ceiling. A small cabinet sat alongside his bunk. The floor was bare but his goose-feathered bed was warm and comfortable.

Many nights Lonely would lie on his bed with nothing but the loud chorus of mountain crickets for company. He thought of Kelzie, how he'd love to see her again. Would she remember him? She'd be taller than him by now for sure. He imagined how beautiful she would be, how she'd wear her ears – up, down, tied back or maybe even plaited. He thought of Mr Flannegan, of Bella, and of Bronson locked up in prison; he wondered where Celia might be. He hadn't heard from any of them since that dreadful night of his escape out of Port Alveridge.

Lonely had learnt so much more about the Felines from the Jukes, and so much more about the Port's mayor. The Jukes knew it all from a different perspective, it seemed. Uncle Jeroboam had guffawed with laughter when Lonely had referred to A. K. Ruddegan as mayor. He stopped Lonely mid-sentence, stared him squarely in the eye and stated bluntly, 'Listen to me, my little Hound, let me make this clear: Ruddegan is NOT the mayor. He's a low-ranking Felinean governor who ain't nothin' but a greedy, gutless puppet, dancing on a Felinean string! What Felineans call the Co-Habitation Treaty, we here in the Shipwoods call the Felinean Occupation. That's what it is, Lonely, an occupation by our age-old Feline enemy from a foreign land.'

Obviously upset, Brother Jeroboam had turned and looked away, trying to mask his emotions. It was beginning to dawn on Lonely that the world was actually quite a different place to the one he had believed it to be as a young Houndling at the Orphanage.

From his room, Lonely would gaze through his small shuttered window that opened west towards Port Alveridge. He spent much time in contemplation, looking out over the hills towards the sea. Coal smoke from five hundred shacks hung heavy in the valley beneath him, like a grey blanket. The ocean was way too far off but he imagined he could almost see it. What lay in the hills between was mostly a mystery to him. He thought of Freedom Swamp and Jenny La Rue and tried to fill in everything in between. He struggled to remember the journey he'd made that eventful night, clinging to his friend Bronson. Maybe, he thought to himself, it was better to not remember it at all. He felt as if he had accidently stumbled into a new chapter of life, one with a purpose. Maybe it was here at Molars Post that he belonged.

But that fateful Tuesday night it was all about to change. The evening's meeting had gone as usual. His new song, 'Liberty Lies Awaiting', backed by the Sunshine Boys, had brought the house down. Little did he know it was prophetic but with a sinister twist.

As Lonely walked home alone he was aware of something different. It wasn't just that it was darker than usual that night as he trudged up Sawpit Road. He suddenly felt vulnerable, unsafe. He quickened his pace and ran to get into the weak pool of yellow light shed by the next street-light. He gasped a chestful of breaths and then ran to the steps leading up to his room. As he opened the door, he sensed it too late. Cats!

A sickening blow hit him from behind. It was dark, then darker still as he was gagged and a sack was pulled down tight over his head.

All Lonely could remember was hearing the words, 'We've got you, dog. Let's hear you sing now!' They wrestled him out the door and into the shadows, where a black saloon was waiting with its boot open. There was a slamming of doors, then a sudden spray of gravel as the car raced away into the woods on the outskirts of town.

Mick, Leroy and Buddy, making their way home to bed, saw the head-lamps switch on some distance down the road, and heard the powerful engine roar into life. An engine like that could only mean one thing. Cats. And Cats being here would have only one thing in mind. Lonely. They ran straight to Uncle Jeroboam but there was little that could be done. There was no way of catching the speeding thugs. They had been outdone. And they had let Lonely down. Surely he too was bound for that rusting hulk upriver – *Miss Liberty*.

As Lonely lay petrified in the boot, wrenched from side to side as the car swerved and cornered at high speed, each bump made his head ache

Shipwood Mountains Open Day

even more. The car finally slowed then stopped. The boot burst open and he was hauled to his feet by the scruff of his neck. As the sack was pulled roughly from his head, he blinked in the early-morning light and found himself eye to unblinking eye with Warden O'Grady. A sadistic smirk stamped all over his face, O'Grady did not even speak, merely let his bulk and closeness intimidate Lonely Dog. Finally O'Grady turned to a large Tom standing by. 'Get him out of my sight!' he snarled, and walked off.

Lonely looked around to see he was standing on the gangway of the notorious prison ship, *Miss Liberty*. He was pushed and shoved up the gangway and then on further, towards the front of the ship. Instead of going down the stairway into the hold with the other prisoners, they jostled him right to the bow.

The large Tom spoke. 'We've been expecting you for way too long, dog! We've prepared a special cell for you. Hope you'll find it to your liking!'

The Toms all roared with malicious laughter. One bent down and lifted a heavy iron hatch that opened to the anchor well. They threw Lonely down onto the pile of rusty chain and slammed the hatch shut. Instantly it became almost completely dark again, save for a sliver of light through the hole that fed the chain down to the anchor. Lonely sat on the great rusty links and sobbed, his head in his hands.

$\sim$

Unbeknown to the little Hound, destiny was still at work.

'It's a strange thing, you know, Luther,' said Larry as he sat on the porch looking thoughtful. 'In all the years I've done the coal run to *Miss Liberty* down at Fever Creek, I've never delivered nothing other than coal. Just today I get a telegram to bring thirteen drums of petrol to the docks. Urgently. It was sent by the Chief Warden. Now don't you think that's strange, Brother Luther? Drums of petrol and all, for a coal-powered steamship?'

'Strange indeed, Larry,' replied Luther. 'Wish we could just use that petrol to blow them mean prison Toms to kingdom come and sail aways to freedom! The Howlers and *Miss Liberty*, her skirts a-flying just like the old glory days.'

Luther stopped with his mouth open. He turned urgently to Larry, and gestured him in close. Quietly he said, 'Larry, I've an idea. Those petrol drums…'

O'Grady had looked on as a group of crew-cut Toms worked in the fetid heat to offload the last of the petrol drums from Larry's truck and into a large cargo net. A rusty crane hoisted the load high over the forward deck and into the hold.

'Just as well you got here early,' O'Grady had said to Larry when his ancient truck had creaked into view, belching smoke. 'I've got a *barbeque* planned tonight. Want to be getting on home to get it ready.'

The creepy way he had emphasized the word barbeque had given Larry the chills. He suspected he knew what O'Grady had planned.

Now, as O'Grady fumbled with the keys to open his car door, he turned and froze, a sickening feeling rising inside him. Walking off the ship towards him were fifteen of the ship-based Tom prison guards, hands cuffed behind their heads, wearing nothing but their underwear, grim-faced and humiliated. Like Noah's ark, the ship's door slammed shut behind them, with not a sign of life anywhere on board.

The watchtower on shore became a hive of activity. The guards were un-cuffed, spare clothing found, weapons issued, and commands shouted. O'Grady remained fixed to the spot, crew-cut bristling, his jaw working hard. He looked from truck to ship. Ship to truck. As comprehension dawned, his eyes closed, and all bluster and bravado went out of him. He saw clearly that he, a major player, had been outplayed.

The drums, so carefully loaded onto the ship, had contained an altogether different form of menace. Instead of petrol, each had held a

Howler, armed and dangerous, and itching to get Lonely Dog and their leader, Bronson, back. This was Luther's master plan – a takeover from the inside. Literally!

His face turning red with a turgid mixture of rage and embarrassment, O'Grady spun on his heels and began yelling orders. There was no way he was going to let a single Hound get off the gangplank onto dry land. He commanded Toms to line both sides of the approach, and had wire, vehicles and old building materials lined up as barricades. They would have to get food and water at some point. When they did, he would be ready. There was no way he was letting his prestigious catch – the great Lonely Dog – elude his grasp.

Hours later, as the day drew to a tense close, there had been not a single sign of activity on board *Miss Liberty*. It was as if she was deserted. Hatches and doors remained shut as tight as a purse. As darkness fell, O'Grady went from Tom to Tom, urging them to greater vigilance and threatening harm to wives and children if they did not successfully recapture Lonely Dog.

At five minutes to midnight, a cry went up from a Tom high in a watchtower. Smoke had begun to billow from the ship's funnel into the velvet-black night sky.

O'Grady could only yell a despairing 'No!'

The word was barely out of his mouth when there was a distant rumbling sound, a hiss and clank that sounded almost like a Houndskiffle rhythm section. *Miss Liberty* was tugging at her mooring lines!

The ship lurched and heaved and the Toms on dry land watched as decks creaked and a guard tower came crashing down, narrowly missing a terrified Warden O'Grady. The Hounds were safe from the Toms' bullets inside the steel hull.

In the boiler room Hound stokers shovelled coal into the furnace as if the Devil himself were on their backs. There was no shortage of coal, for even as a prison ship *Miss Liberty* drew her power from the old steam engines down below. But the Hounds had hardly dared hope their stoking could make the old lady move!

It had been many years since Luther had last seen the engine of *Miss Liberty* and the state of the pistons and the camshaft made him shake his head. He remembered the bilges and engine room of his old ship

Beaconsfield

well and got straight to the task of making her mobile. Eventually, to the Hounds' amazement, their toil was rewarded. *Miss Liberty* finally gave a wild, decisive shudder, smashed the jetty to matchsticks, wrenched the mooring lines free and steamed out into the pea-green waters of Fever Creek.

'So, where are we headed?' grinned Bronson.

'Beaconsfield!' Luther pointed south. 'The Baron's waiting for us with his Houndsford Motorized Battalion!'

Bronson and Lonely stood on the prow, ears flapping, as the giant smoke-stacks above the Cannery hove into sight. The ship steamed at full speed through Fisherton Basin, past cheering crowds lining the viaduct, and on out to sea. They were free! Everyone gathered in the ship's mess, and the celebrations began. To chants of 'Lonely! Lonely!' the little Hound was lifted high onto a table. A guitar was thrust into his hands. Apart from the dull throbbing of the engine, the room became completely silent. In a voice choked with emotion Lonely began to sing.

> Liberty lies awaiting,
> Freedom's slipped her chain,
> Ready to take their riders,
> They won't be back again.

On they sailed, the chimneys growing smaller, the lights of Port Alver-idge growing fainter, until darkness enveloped the sea and the outlaw ship.

honstadt's Castle

Och y'ell nair take me alive
Not on these Hills
The Hills thart I cull Home
Y'ell nair chain me nor subdue me
NO!
Not without a fight!
For every time ye cut me down
The sod and soil will call
And on these bloody Hills of Home
Another will stand tall!

—Battle Song of the Highland Hounds,
penned by Flagon McOffal

*T*he Baron of Beaconsfield had never learned to play the bagpipes, though this never deterred him. So, on the evening when *Miss Liberty* came steaming round Idle Heads and into Beacons Bay, he took the chanter in his arms, pumped the bag with his elbow and blew into the mouthpiece as if it were the Judgement Day trumpet.

Lining the decks of the prison ship, the convict Hounds stared in wonderment. If the sight of the Baron in his kilt perched on the battlements of his castle was not enough, the sound that wailed from his pipes certainly was. At first they mistook the caterwauling for an animal being tortured, but as they listened there could be no doubt that this was music of a sort. The Baron was greeting them with a traditional Houndish dirge.

> Ye'll come back nah
> Ye'll come nah hume
> Over the sea ye'll come

And I'll be here ma luv

Awaitin' for thee

When ye cum nah hume ta me!

Set on a hill overlooking the bay, Beaconsfield Castle was a medieval fortress constructed by the Baron's distant forebear, Boris Rhondstadt, to withstand centuries of invaders, sieges and bombardments. Cannons lined the massive stone walls, crimson flags snapped in the wind, and there was a full complement of turrets as well as an impressive guardhouse manned by Howlers.

Inside the wheelhouse, Luther cranked the brass lever to full throttle. There was a last-minute flurry of activity in the engine room as stokers furiously shovelled coal into the furnace. The prisoners on the decks

Alveridge Hall, Beaconsfield

braced themselves. As the gap between ship and shore rapidly closed, the bow of the rusty hulk finally lurched upwards to a shuddering halt. The good ship *Miss Liberty* had delivered her last cargo, arriving at her final resting place high and dry on the gravel beach at Beacons Bay.

As Lonely followed the Hounds off *Miss Liberty* and up the stony track to the castle, his eye was caught by something rising into the sky that was clearly not medieval. On the very top of Beacon Rock stood a towering pylon topped with a huge dish made up of hundreds of rusty sheets of corrugated iron and with a bulbous contraption like a chess piece at its centre. Painted across the monstrous dish were the words 'Beaconsfield Radio'. This, Lonely realized, was the transmitter through which the Baron broadcast his daily tirades, his bagpipe dirges,and the Houndish folk ballads about battles won and Cats defeated.

That evening five hundred ravenous Hounds filled the long tables of the Baron's Great Hall, which groaned with a sumptuous banquet: plump speckled-goose, pigs' heads stuffed with marzipan-sculpted Cats, plat-ters of pungent haggish (spotty russock stuffed with minced strudel-hen, soaked for ten days in simmering whale milk). At the top table, the Baron, in full regalia, ensured that his Wilks beer flowed like the Juke River in May. Speeches were made, toasts proposed, songs rose into the crisp, starry night.

In the dungeons in the bowels of the castle, some two dozen Toms – former prison guards from the *Liberty* – listened to the merriment in forlorn silence. And high in the tallest turret, in the spartan room that was his cell, another prisoner listened too.

Howlers' Hangout

Rolph Flannegan upended a bottle of Triple Malted Snarler and a single drop splashed into his glass. He tossed it aside and scoured his cell for another, finally finding one that still had a mouthful left in it, under the sagging sofa. He sank to the floor, glugging thankfully, then sat for a long time, letting the whisky burn his gut and soothe his soul. Eventually he got up and stumbled to the door. It was locked. He banged on it uselessly, weak with grief and booze.

On the other side, a Howler standing guard called, 'You behave yourself now, Flannegan! What do you want?'

Rolph Flannegan slumped down and leaned against the door. There were so many things he wanted, chief among them to roll back time and undo his many sins.

He'd known his time was up when Bronson had stepped off the liberated prison ship earlier that day. Bronson had wasted no time in telling the Baron of Flannegan's betrayal, accusing his old headmaster of taking money from Mayor Ruddegan in return for spying on his Hound friends. The Baron had been stunned. He could not believe that his oldest friend was involved in such skulduggery, but the evidence proved irrefutable.

Old Rolph had mumbled excuses and pitiful explanations but to no avail. As one Hound, the assembled Howlers and the Baron himself had literally turned their backs on their old friend. In keeping with Houndish tradition, Rolph was then made to walk the traitor's walk through their ranks before being led to the cramped turret room that was to be his cell while they pondered what to do with him.

Of all the Hounds, only Lonely had turned to look as his old headmaster passed. The hurt and betrayal Rolph glimpsed in those sad eyes were greater punishment than any that could be inflicted on him.

When the Howler called again, 'What do you want?', Rolph knew the answer should be 'Forgiveness and redemption in the eyes of my friends and companions!', but instead he heard his slurred voice mutter, 'Whisky! I need more whisky!'

CHAPTER XXIII

Curries and curfews

I believe in Angels
Whisper of Wind, Shimmy of Light
Glory in Gold, Cloaked with the Night.
Messengers, Minstrels, Mellifluous Beings
I believe in Angels
Oft without seeing.

—Trad Houndish Hymn,
from the *Collected Works of the Rev Trent Kneebender*

*B*ella lugged a heavy pot of fish-head stew off the
stove and began ladling the glutinous mixture into chipped
bowls on the rough wooden kitchen table. A dozen orphans
in ragged overalls licked their lips, eyeing each spoonful.

'I'm sorry, my dears, but it's fish-head stew again tonight.'

The Houndlings ate hungrily, licking their bowls, their spoons, their
fingers. Bella watched, holding back the tears that seemed to flow so
easily these days.

It was a long time since she'd thought of the Orphanage, and her
kitchen there. When it had closed and she had tried desperately to
find homes for her orphans, she had never dreamed she would end up
taking in more youngsters. But there were always more Houndlings that
needed help. Especially since the 'Emergency Powers' Mayor Ruddegan
had enacted in the wake of the escape of the convict Hounds aboard
Miss Liberty. Strict curfews were now imposed in Port Alveridge and
hundreds of Toms had been trucked in to enforce them. The Howlers

Feline Gossips Ruling the Town

Motorcycle Gang had been outlawed and there was a price on Bronson's head. Anyone found harbouring or assisting Fever Creek escapees was to be shipped off to rot in a stone fortress in Felinea known as the Pit.

Hounds everywhere were out of work as businesses folded under the draconian provisions. No bars could open after 5 p.m., nor any restaurants or cafés on weekday evenings; fishing boats couldn't set out from the Port without Tom security personnel on board; public performances of Houndskiffle and blues were banned for fear of inciting unlawful behaviour; and Revellers Green was off limits, ringed with barricades and barbed-wire fences.

For some time now, Bella had been working as a dish washer in a bustling curry house down by the wharf called 'Inside the Sun'. The owner,

Syd Snarlington, an old Hound crippled by his addiction to curry, alcohol and wandering hands, had offered her two cramped attic rooms and two hot meals a day in exchange for working for free in the restaurant. Since his arthritis kept him from climbing the steep stairs to the attic, Syd was not aware that Bella had taken in a dozen orphan Houndlings, who slept around the kitchen stove and – when Syd was sober, which thankfully was rarely – tried to keep quiet.

There was someone else who shared Bella's cramped attic rooms. Kelzie. Now she stood up to her elbows in dishwater as the Houndlings stacked plates on the bench beside her. 'Hurry up and get ready for bed!' she chided and they scampered to get the best position around the fire.

Ever since the Orphanage was sold, Kelzie had been Bella's right-hand Hound – and, truth be told, her left hand too. Bella was getting frailer. She had had no news of her wayward son, Marvin, since his release from Trumaine Borstal, nor any word from Rolph Flannegan, though she knew he was now a broken Hound living under the Baron's roof in Beaconsfield. Without two Alvers to rub together, Bella Bostock was no longer equal to the strain of having so many little ones to feed and clothe. Only Kelzie made it possible for them to survive.

Kelzie wiped her hands and shushed the Houndlings. Catching a glimpse of herself in the cracked kitchen window pane, she stared at the image it reflected back – the lank hair, the stained dress, the hands wrinkled from months of dishwater.

'You're beautiful, my sweetheart!' whispered Bella, watching Kelzie. 'Any Hound would be lucky to have you.'

Kelzie dabbed her eyes and turned away.

'Come on, you lot!' she said. 'Get settled before the radio goes on or you'll miss the show.'

'Or she'll miss her boyfriend!' a cheeky Houndling said.

Kelzie blushed beetroot red and Bella clipped the Houndling round the ears. 'That will be enough of that talk, Ephus! Mr Lonely Dog is an old and dear friend of Miss Kelzie's and mine.'

The little radio on the bookshelf buzzed and crackled as Kelzie adjusted the dial. Suddenly the Baron's distinctive voice broke through:

'…and I will continue to stem the tide of foul Felines with every last drop of my Houndish blood! That concludes our Cooking Hour.

'Now a much anticipated part of our nightly programming, some music to stir your very souls, from the small Hound with the big voice, that some call a renegade and others call a hero…'

There came a deep voice, matured with age, softened by experience, but unmistakable.

'Good evening, my name is Lonely Dog!'

Kelzie's heart leapt, the Houndlings tittered, Bella wept.

Across the Port, in his opulent mayoral offices, A. K. Ruddegan picked up a crystal vase and hurled it at the radio. 'Lonely Dog! Why can't you bumbling fools find him and make sure he truly is Lonely?'

Cyrus, the head of Ruddegan's Internal Security Force, was unmoved by the Mayor's fury. The heavyset Tom with cold blue eyes swivelled in the red leather chair.

'As you know, Mr Mayor, he's holed up in Beaconsfield and until we get significant reinforcements we won't—'

'Significant reinforcements?' screamed Ruddegan. He slammed his fist on the desk, flecks of spittle streaking his whiskers, his eyes glowing with rage. 'What about the truckloads of Toms pouring into this town? What are they doing? Playing jazz?'

'I won't dignify that with an answer.' Cyrus rose and made to leave. At the door he turned and stared back at Ruddegan, who was panting alarmingly.

'Besides, you have more to worry about than resistance fighters and their rebel radio.'

Ruddegan glowered at him uncertainly. 'What are you saying?'

'Celia, your granddaughter,' said Cyrus in an icy tone, 'has disappeared from St Bilius Convent and was last seen heading this way.'

'Here? To Port Alveridge?'

'To Beaconsfield!' The Security Chief's eyes glittered with cold menace. 'And my orders are to stop her – by any means necessary!' He stepped outside and let the door swing shut. Ruddegan stared after him in horror.

⁓

It had taken two years of thinking, months of planning and much painful claw-work for Celia to execute her plan to escape Felinea. Getting out of the soundless cloisters of St Bilius Convent, where she was under surveillance from morning until bedtime, had involved countless nights spent secretly scraping mortar from between the medieval stones, leaving her claws blunt and bleeding. Once outside in the vast, dark night, she had been careful to move quietly, dodging the heavily guarded border stations and Tom patrols as she headed south towards the coast. She had

Whalemilkers Head Out from Port Alveridge

lain low for two cold nights under the pier before managing to stow away to Narmel aboard an old steamer carrying a cargo of Turkmesh carpets and Catalonian catnip to Port Alveridge. From the deck she had been alarmed to see a flotilla of sleek black Felinean battleships also headed south.

In the weeks before her escape, the air had been abuzz with rumours of war. It had also been abuzz with something else – music! The music of Lonely Dog. Every night in her stark bedroom-cell in St Bilius, Celia had put on her headphones and tuned her tiny crystal radio to the rebel stations broadcasting from the Shipwoods, and recently to Beaconsfield Live, to hear Lonely Dog sing.

She was not the only Cat listening. All across Felinea young Cats in their thousands were holed up in their bedrooms, twiddling the dials of their illicit radios and tuning into Lonely's music, beamed live from Beaconsfield Castle and bounced across the mountains and the miles by rebel transmitters. At first, older Cats, and indeed the Authorities, had regarded this aberration as teenage Cat behaviour – a determination by the younger generation to reject their parents' musical tastes. But when it continued, they took the precaution of banning listening to 'crass Hound music', sought out and smashed the covert radio sets and hoped that this would suffice. But it did not.

Like the head of the Medusa, with every listener that was cut off, two more appeared. Lonely's music had struck a chord that transcended breed and creed, a chord that resonated deep within young Cats raised in the stultifying confines of Felinean culture. Lonely's songs spoke of freedom gained and love lost, of injustice and pain, but above all of making a stand. Of rising up.

Night after night his voice became their voice, his songs their songs, until they spilled out from under the pillows, out from the closets and locked bedrooms, down the stairs past startled parents, and out on to the streets of Felinea.

By the time the Authorities finally took action it was too late, and no amount of radio burnings or threats and beatings could change that. Young Cats openly defied the law, dancing to Lonely's music in Felinean nightclubs, buying bootleg recordings on the thriving black market. Soon songs like 'Look Me in the Eye' were booming from café radios across downtown Catside.

Look me in the eye, Mama

And tell me you don't know

Why the tide is turning

Why the rivers overflow

'Cause everything is changing

Everything's brand new

Now look me in the eye

And tell me you can't see it too!

The Powers and the Generals in Felinea realized that they had a rebellion on their hands. They had to quash it quickly and ruthlessly before it undermined all that was Feline. Lonely Dog and the rebel-rousing Hounds had to be stopped, his music forever silenced, the radio transmitters that broadcast his vile filth blown to Catdom Come.

Plans were drawn up, alliances forged. The Powers looked about them for a scapecat and turned to the little town of Port Alveridge, to its ineffectual mayor, A. K. Ruddegan. It was only fair, the Generals decided, that he should bear the blame. After all, his failure to destroy the transmitters had directly led to this untenable situation. Port Alveridge would be liberated by battalions of the 1st Felinicus Assault Regiment, Ruddegan would be replaced and, having crushed Houndside, the army would march on Beaconsfield to be met by a fleet of battleships from the Felinean Naval Squadron. The Baron and his rebels would learn the price of rebellion. Their bodies would be strung up in the Tumbleroot trees of Revellers Green, and Lonely Dog and the Baron would swing from the highest branches!

Such were the rumours Celia had overheard in her long nights clawing mortar, from the room next door where the St Bilius dormitory matron was conducting an illicit affair with a fat Felinean colonel. It was these rumours that had urged her on as she opened a small hole in the stone wall of her cell, clambered down knotted bed sheets and travelled alone, by night, across Felinea, a rebel in her own land. She had to get to Beaconsfield and warn Lonely Dog.

Now, as she crept from the cargo ship through the docks at Port Alveridge, she was at least back in familiar territory. She moved stealthily through the Port, ducked under the tangle of razor wire that had been Revellers Green, and found – where the Howlers had left it – a sleek black Houndster. She had feared the Tom patrols would have discovered it, but it still languished, unused, under the garish tarpaulin painted like a rocking horse.

Celia had never ridden a motorbike before, but she was a quick learner and in a few short minutes she wheeled it up Tumbleton Avenue, where no one would be able to hear, kicked it roaring into life and headed for the hills, towards the Baron's estate, where no lone Cat had ever dared venture before. A cold wind scythed in from the sea, across the growing dark.

After miles of dust and having carefully navigated the twists and turns of Hell-Riders Canyon in the bike's dim headlight, Celia finally breathed a sigh of relief as she drove the throbbing Houndster round the last corner. The lights of Beaconsfield Castle shone alone and defiant in the inky void before her, the huge transmitter floodlit behind it. She quickly cut the engine, killing the headlight. Though hungry, cold and half dead

Tumbleton Avenue

with exhaustion, Celia smiled. As she stood shivering by a twisted Knobb tree, clutching its spindly trunk for balance, she stared at the enormous illuminated beacon and pondered her next step.

Some part of Lonely died the day that old Rolph was locked away. In the months that followed, Lonely felt as much a prisoner as old Rolph, spending most of his days in his own turret room and coming down only for his nightly broadcasts on the radio. There, in the small stone radio studio just off the Baron's library, with only a Hound technician for company, he performed with the lights dimmed, trying to conjure the faces of friends so he could sing just for them. He did not know or care who else might be listening. Gone was the jubilation of breaking free with Bronson and the others from Fever Creek, gone was the thrill of performing in the Cathedral of Rock at Molars Post. Now when he played he felt only a numbing sadness, the desolate absence of that one thing that had brought him so far. Hope.

The songs he wrote in those bleak months were filled with a pain and sorrow he struggled to express. The chords he knew felt inadequate so he tinkered with the steam-powered amp Brother Jeroboam had given him, to startling and unique effect. Sometimes the castle would shudder with these experiments. The Baron would shake his head and Bronson would chuckle, but in his heart the big Hound worried to see Lonely retreating to the solitude of his Orphanage years, the self-imposed loneliness. And Bronson knew the answer lay in the tower cell, guarded night and day, cowering and crying. Yet things were stirring in the heavens that no one could anticipate.

CHAPTER XXIV

Radio-Hams and Renegades

Justice wears a blindfold
That's why I wear a chain
She's blinded to my innocence
She's blinded to my pain.
I'm serving twenty long ones
For somethin' I did not do
But Justice wears a blindfold
And my coffin lid is screwed.

—Lonely Dog, *Live at Fever Creek*
(Convicted Hound Bootleg Recordings)

*T*here are those who believe the lives of
Hounds are governed by nothing more than the ebb
and flow of the Esparrow Sea and the blooming of
Cherry-Whistle trees in spring. Others would say
that their lives are the result of a dice game played
by Fate, a roll of chance, luck not Providence.

In her nightly prayers, down on her swollen knees and wrapped in her
threadbare gown, Bella disagreed. She stared out beyond the leaking roof
of Syd Snarlington's attic, up into the starry vault above Port Alveridge,
all the way to that place in the fiery cosmos of faith where hope is born.

As Bella staggered painfully to her feet and slipped into her cold bed,
her whispered prayers, carried on the hope in which she wrapped them,
must have soared to the Provident Being she had believed in for so long.
For that night, as the Port lay asleep; as Celia, cold and shivering, climbed
up the craggy rock face towards the Baron's castle; as in his dim radio
studio Lonely sang to an audience he had never seen; as Bronson and the

Baron smoked silently before a roaring fire; and as the armies of Felinea were poised to strike; Providence intervened.

Surely the simple prayers of an ageing Hound cannot move the hand of Providence? But as Bella curled up in her chilly bed that night, a blue glow crept over her windowsill, waking her with a start. Bella Bostock sat up and stared as the room filled with a glorious blue light, then she leapt up with the energy of a youngster and went to waken her Houndlings.

Ruddegan too saw the blue halo of light rising like a saint from prayer in the northern sky. A chill ran down his spine as he reached for the phone.

Lying on the floor of his room, surrounded by the detritus of his drunkenness, old Rolph felt the touch of the blue light through his tormented dreams and woke, struggled to his feet and stood blinking in the promise of its redemptive glow.

Staring into the flames as the Baron nodded off in his armchair, Bronson heard a sentry on the battlements call his name. He roused the Baron and the two raced up the spiral staircase and stood, astonished, as the sentry pointed from the balcony to the shimmering, almost super-natural glow over the Esparrow Sea.

The Blue Moon had returned.

Celia saw the blue glow reflected in the faces of the sentries who were standing in a trance near the guardhouse. She had drafted and redrafted her plans for entering the invincible fortress, built to withstand an army of invading Cats, let alone one friendly Feline. She worried that she'd fail to convince the Howlers standing guard of her true intentions. What if she couldn't deliver the message? What if they simply seized her and threw her into the dungeons without seeking out Bronson or Lonely to vouch for her?

But in the radiant halo of the rising Blue Moon, all her worries were unfounded. She stole past guards held in its glow, stalked past groups of Hounds who did not notice her scent, did not hear the small twigs cracking as she passed. She tiptoed through the main gate, thrown wide so the beam of moonlight could pass through, sidled along a corridor to a heavy door, opened it gently, her heart pounding, and stepped into the room beyond.

Of all the Hounds, only Lonely was oblivious to the Blue Moon rising, since he was tucked away in the dark radio studio, headphones clamped over his long ears, eyes closed tightly, strumming his guitar.

The technician in the adjacent control booth, hearing the cries of alarm and wonder, had long since bolted, but Lonely did not notice.

'I'd like to do one more number before I let you all get some sleep,' he said quietly into the microphone. 'It's by an old musical hero of mine, Van Trong, and I hope you like it.'

> I seen the Generals in their smoky rooms
> Plotting and planning every young Hound's doom
> They'll be marching to battle pretty soon
> When will the wars all end?

As he began the chorus, he imagined he heard a voice in his head singing harmony with him, a familiar voice, a voice from long ago…

So tell me, when will the wars all end?

When will they lay down their guns?

When will peace be the message we send?

Can you tell me the answer to that, my friend

When will the wars all end?

Lonely opened his eyes and found himself staring into Celia's face, pressed against the other side of the control-room window. As if in a dream, he reached out to touch her hands through the glass. They went on singing until the song was done, then Lonely ripped off his headphones and rushed into the control booth.

'Celia! What are you doing here?'

She opened her mouth to speak but Lonely was staring past her to a dim sapphire light seeping under the studio door.

'The Blue Moon?' he queried, turning to the doorway. 'It must be the Blue Moon!' But he did not feel the heart-pumping excitement of his younger days, did not feel the urge to run and see it. He turned back to Celia.

'I… I thought you were… sent away? How did you get here? Why did you come here… all this way?'

'I came to warn you, Lonely.'

'Warn me?'

'Your music has stirred up big trouble back in Felinea.'

'Who listens to my music in Felinea?'

'Modest as ever! Why should your words not speak to Cats as well as Hounds?'

'Cats?'

'Yes, Cats! Young Cats everywhere have been tuning in to your broadcasts; I listened to you every night in my room at the convent. It's what kept me sane.' She squeezed his hand. 'But the Powers plan to stop you for good.'

'What can they do?' Lonely's eyes narrowed.

'They're mobilizing an army as we speak! They plan to crush Port Alveridge and Beaconsfield, but it's you and the Baron they're after. That's what I came to tell you. You have to run, Lonely, go back to the Shipwoods.'

'I will not run again!' Lonely whispered hoarsely.

Celia cupped his face in her hands. 'If you don't leave tonight, they will silence you forever. I've seen the warships heading south from Felinea, and soldiers in the streets.'

'There was a time when I would've run.' Lonely stared into Celia's emerald eyes. 'But I'm tired of running, tired of being a fugitive in my own country. Let them come! I'll take my chances.'

'Oh, you'll take your chances?' Celia bristled. 'You and the rabble the Baron calls an army? You'll march up into the hills of Beaconsfield like the armies of old, Cat and Hound slaughtering each other until the rivers stain the Esparrow Sea, then bury the dead and start all over again? Is that what you want, Lonely? Is it? What about the world you sang about, what about peace and freedom? Were they just words you needed to make a rhyme? Hounds and Cats believe in what you sing, they believe in *you*! Stay if you must, but for the sake of those who believe in you, you've got to stand up and stop this carnage. Get back on the radio and tell them what's happening! Rally them, under this Blue Moon! Lead them!'

She sank on to the couch, exhausted.

'Listen to me, my dear Celia.' Lonely took her gently by the shoulders. 'I sing songs and play guitar. That's it. I'm no leader, I'm just Arthur Snout, a lonely orphan who found he could say things in song he would never dare say in plain words. Sometimes I feel like everybody wants me to do something, be something, sing something, but I just want to be left alone, Celia. I don't want to be more than I am: a Hound with a guitar and a pocketful of songs. I guess what I'm trying to say is I'm no Van Trong; I never will be!'

There was a sudden movement by the doorway, a figure staggering into the dim pool of light.

It was Rolph Flannegan.

∾

As the light of the Blue Moon had spilled into Rolph's room, he had stood in its glare and thought of those he'd loved and hurt down the years. He saw himself back in the Orphanage classroom, with Bella in her kitchen, saw himself beneath the Tumbleroot on Revellers Green, playing his guitar, saw himself with a young Houndette in a gypsy dress lying in the sun.

Suddenly the Blue Moon seemed to burn with fire. Rolph cried out and fell to his knees, sobbing, begging 'Forgive me!' over and over again, reaching across the valley of time, into the abyss of his past.

When he got to his feet again, weak of knee and wringing wet, he felt for the first time in years something rising within his soul, something so startling, so unexpected, that for a while he could not put a name to it.

It was peace.

The guard outside Rolph's door had deserted his post to go and watch the Blue Moon rising. Rolph took a step back, braced himself and charged the door. It splintered open, sending the old Hound crashing into the stone wall beyond. Blood trickled down his hand and he felt a stab of pain but he plunged on down the stairs regardless. He had to find Lonely.

～

With a long, elegantly manicured finger nail, Ruddegan speared a goldfish from the bowl and swallowed it whole, sloshed a full five measures of gin into a tumbler and downed it, refilled the glass and washed down a handful of painkillers. He hadn't slept or eaten in days and his head felt as if a herd of bulls in hobnails were running through it. The office clock chimed midnight and he hurled the empty tumbler at it, smashing the glass front.

He turned and glowered down the mahogany conference table at a dozen Toms seated nervously along its length. They had never seen the Mayor so unhinged, and it worried them. All except Cyrus, who paid Ruddegan's histrionics no heed.

It was Cyrus who had suggested the Mayor call this midnight meeting to implement a plan of action for dealing with the sudden appearance of the Blue Moon.

'Need I remind you, Mr Mayor,' he purred menacingly, 'that the Authorities in Felinea will be watching this new development keenly. They will expect you to keep your Hounds on a very short lead.'

Ruddegan sent the goldfish bowl crashing to the floor.

'There is not a leash strong enough in Alveridgea to hold back the Hounds when the Blue Moon shines! They'll head to Marmalade Mountain like wasps to truffle honey and there's not a damned thing I can do about it.'

'We must be seen to be maintaining law and order, Mr Mayor,' Cyrus replied icily, 'Blue Moon or not.'

Ruddegan whirled on Cyrus, eyeing him balefully. When he finally spoke, it was with disdain. 'So tell me, Cyrus, as you seem to be the expert in these matters, how exactly would you enforce the law with ten thousand Hounds on the loose?'

'Firstly,' Cyrus stood and moved to a map of the Port, 'announce the cancellation of all Blue Moon festivities. Secondly, impose a total curfew – no Hound to leave their home day or night for the duration of the Blue Moon. Any Hound caught breaking this new curfew to be immediately despatched to the Pit. We have three thousand Toms at our disposal, more than enough to contain the curs of Port Alveridge!'

Ruddegan slumped back in his leather chair, ran his fingers through his dishevelled whiskers. Cyrus's plan would be like poking a hornets' nest with a stick. The Hounds would revolt. There would be blood in the streets – his streets! To deny a Hound access to Marmalade Mountain during the Blue Moon festival was like denying a Kitterling its mother's milk.

'Even a legion of armed Toms won't keep the Hounds in check,' Ruddegan said morosely.

'My thoughts exactly, Mr Mayor.' Cyrus smiled. 'Thoughts shared by our friends in Felinea, which is why they have marshalled the entire army and the navy on our land and sea borders this very night. Let the Hounds whimper and beg! By this time tomorrow all protest will have been suppressed by our invading force. The Blue Moon will mark their destruction!'

'Why was I not informed of this?' Ruddegan's eyes bulged hideously.

'It was privileged information.' Cyrus spat on the floor. 'And you are no longer in a position of privilege, Ruddegan.'

'*Mayor* Ruddegan to you!' he snarled back.

'Ah… another piece of privileged information you have not yet heard. The Powers are tired of you, Ruddegan. You have promised much and delivered little. So, Mayor, Colonel, Colonel-Mayor or whatever your preferred title is today, your role is to be replaced!'

'Replaced!' Ruddegan spluttered. 'By what?'

'By the office of Governor!' Cyrus replied, waving a hand at the office door. The entire room turned to see a Tom fitting a new nameplate on Ruddegan's door. It read: 'GOVERNOR CYRUS'.

uilt, Secrets and Legends

The truth may set you free, but it don't
mean you wanna step outa your cell.

—Missin' Tooth Memphis, intro to
'Two Slugs of Whisky and a Half Glass of Truth'

*R*olph stumbled into the studio, blinking in
the low light. His glasses had got smashed and
without them he was virtually blind.

'Mr Flannegan?'

He heard Lonely's voice, full of astonishment and alarm.

'Arthur? Is that really you, lad?' Rolph reached out to touch him.

'Your hand,' Lonely said, 'it's bleeding.'

'A scratch,' Rolph lied. 'Nothing serious. I've been looking for you,
lad.'

'I don't understand. What are you doing here?'

Rolph hesitated, his hands fell to Lonely's shoulders. 'Who is this with
you, lad?' he asked, raising his grey snout towards Celia.

'A friend,' said Celia simply.

'A Cat friend,' Rolph said quietly, squinting at Lonely. 'Can she be
trusted?'

'I would trust her with my life,' came Lonely's reply. 'Unlike some…'

'Unlike me.' The old Hound smiled weakly. 'I have done nothing to merit your trust, nor even your friendship. But I sought you out so that I might at least ask something of you.'

'We don't have time for riddles,' said Lonely. 'The Blue Moon is rising and Bronson and the Baron will be back any minute. If they find you here they'll throw you out and then where will you go? What is it you want of me?'

Rolph gripped Lonely's shoulder as if he was drowning. 'You have shown me more kindness than I have ever deserved. But don't try to protect this foolish old Hound any more, Arthur. If I am to be cast out of Beaconsfield, out of Alveridgea, so be it. But I must ask you for one thing.'

Sir Peppersford Trousers

Lonely took the old Hound's hands and clasped them tightly. 'Name it.'

Rolph's body suddenly quaked with sobs so fearful that Lonely too was shaken.

'What is it, Mr Flannegan? Tell me what you want.'

Rolph sank to the floor, lifted his grizzled snout to the heavens and cried out in a voice that rose up from the darkest realms of his being.

'Forgiveness, lad! I want your forgiveness!'

There was a long silence, broken only by the sound of Rolph's laboured breathing.

Lonely knelt beside him. 'Maybe it's Bronson or the Baron you should be asking for forgiveness,' Lonely said gently.

Rolph looked up as if he were coming out of a dream.

'There are many from whom I should ask forgiveness, but none more than you, Arthur. You I have failed the most, you and your father.'

'My father? I have no father.'

'Everyone has a father, Arthur.' Rolph looked him in the eye. 'And your father would have been so proud of you.'

'What do you know about my father?'

Rolph stumbled to his feet and stood unsteadily, like a Hound on a cliff-top thinking of jumping, wrestling with demons. Then a great peace washed over him, his shoulders relaxed, he gave a huge sigh and stepped back from the cliff.

'Your father was my son, Arthur. My only son. His name was also Arthur. Arthur Van Trong!'

Lonely stood stock still. Not a muscle moved. Speechless.

Celia staggered back against the couch. Then, finding her voice again, she leapt forward and grabbed Rolph's collar. 'You crazy old drunk! I know you! I've seen you around my grandfather's office. You betrayed your own kind for a handful of cash. You're as rotten as he is. Now here you are telling your stinking lies to Lonely.'

Rolph listened with unnerving patience until she had no more to say. Then, in a whisper, as though to himself, he began to talk.

'When I was young, the age you both are now, I went to sea as a sailor and stayed away for many years. On my return, I climbed a hill above Port Alveridge and sat down beneath a Tumbleroot tree. The Esparrow was as green as a snuffle-beak's egg and all the world seemed born new. I took up my guitar and let the music flow until I was lost inside it. That's when she came – from where I never knew. In a gypsy skirt she climbed the hill and found me. Together we sat in the shade of the tree and the roots enveloped us. I enveloped her and she me, the sun warm on our backs. I have seen her many times since in my dreams.

'It was not until many months later that I knew she had had a pup, a son, our son. She called him Arthur and gave him her family name, Van Trong. She it was who raised him while I, foolishly, watched from afar, ashamed to speak, ashamed of the act that had conceived my own flesh and blood.

'I was set on becoming a scholar then, and the respect of my peers mattered more to me than the respect of my own son. He never knew me, but I watched him grow into manhood, watched him marry a sweet Hound from Cripplecat Creek, watched them have a pup – a Houndling they called Arthur. Oh, I longed to hold you in my arms, Arthur, but my secret had taken root.

'I know now that even the deepest secrets can be wormed out by one who seeks them. Your grandfather, Celia, scavenges for secrets. He knew me as a militant during the years I spent living in Felinea. Like a young fool, I had bought into the ideologies of the Felineans. I believed the lie that a supreme power could unite us all. I thought the Felineans would succeed. Instead, the Baron led the Hounds to victory and defeated their advances on our shores. At the same time came new negotiations: King Alver II signed the Co-Habitation Treaty, which opened our lands to the Felinean Occupation and has since grown into something far more sinister, the beginning of the Felinean dictatorship that we know today.

'I knew I had made a terrible mistake, and realized I had betrayed my own kind and turned my back on my own flesh and blood. Your grand-father, Celia, knew I defected all those years back and that all the battles, all the reflected glory, were lies.

'All that would have been enough to crush me. But Ruddegan also used my son against me, the fruit of youthful passion. He blackmailed me, threatened to expose everything if I didn't do his bidding and spy on my fellow Hounds. I was to leak inside information about the folks around him. Like a card player revealing the hand of another, so he could manipulate the town for his own ends. I fed him information, most of it not very helpful. Deeply compromised, I tried hard to never give much away. But in his hands it became lethal.

'He assuaged my guilt with money. At first I clung to the illusion that I took the cash only for the Orphanage, but gradually he reeled me in, a hapless fish, snared on the hook of greed. It seems I still haven't learnt my lesson, all these years later. Ruddegan blackmailed me to reveal Bronson's whereabouts. He promised that if he had Bronson he would leave you alone, Arthur. I betrayed Bronson, believing it was my only hope to save you. I should have known better.

'But back in those days I still had a glow of pride. I was proud of my son, who grew from a humble songwriter into a passionate leader of the downtrodden, into a Hound who championed all the things that I also came to believe in. His goal was something far greater than a change of power. He believed it was only a change of heart, in both Hounds and Felines alike, that could unite us. He was right. I was proud to see working Hounds rally to his cause, proud to know that perhaps, where I had failed, my son might succeed in bringing about a more just society, a new equality between Hounds and Cats.

'I was there watching from a nearby hill the night my son led the protest at the Cannery, there when he played to the crowd. I feared Ruddegan's Toms would come – my son must have expected that too. I thought maybe a rogue Tom might rough up a few protesters, nothing more. But from that swanky Cat-pit office of his, Ruddegan killed my son. He planned the fire. He made it look like a careless Hound had accidentally started it with his torch. Collateral damage and a charred Cannery warehouse were a small price to pay to rid himself of his opposition.

'When I saw the black sedans pull up at the Cannery I knew there would be trouble, knew there was nothing I could do. Fearing the worst, I fled to Cripplecat Creek, where you and your mother lived. I arrived just as they were setting the clapboard farmhouse ablaze. The flames were too fierce, I couldn't reach your mother. Just before the roof collapsed, she thrust a bundle at me through the fire, swaddled in a blanket. It was you, Arthur.

'With you held tight, I raced back to the Orphanage and in the chaos and horror of that night no one saw me. I wrote a simple note, tied it round your neck and placed you in a shoebox on the Orphanage doorstep. Then I slipped upstairs to wash the soot and smoke from my face and clothes. It wasn't until later that night that the Baron delivered the news of what had befallen your father.

'Sweet Bella believed that the angels delivered you to her doorstep and in a way I suppose they did. I watched you grow, always careful not to let the world see the aching affection that filled my soul. When you discovered Van Trong's records in the attic, when you started to dress like him, I thought my heart would break. I almost told you the truth that night we drove back from the Green on my Houndster.

'I have lost every one of those I should have saved. I do not expect you to forgive me, Arthur, nor even understand what I have done. All I have ever wanted is to tell you the truth. Now it is done.'

Lonely had not moved an inch during Rolph's speech. He stared into the distance, past the old Hound, transfixed by what he had just heard. Rolph was about to speak again, but Celia gestured him to be quiet. The old Hound stepped back into the shadows, the door slammed shut and Celia watched as he stumbled into the night.

The Blue Moon infused his departing with a surreal glow.

She turned back towards Lonely. 'The Blue Moon is rising, we must—'

But the studio was empty. Lonely Dog was gone.

lack Frigates on the Horizon

Guilt is like a Tumbleroot tree
The roots of both are buried deep
And who can tell how deep they go
Or when they will turn and upward grow

—Hound Proverb

*B*ronson and the Baron stood on the
battlements staring across the iridescent Esparrow.
The rising sapphire orb held them in thrall.

'Seven times in my life I've witnessed this moon,' the Baron murmured, 'and yet each time is like the first. Every Hound that draws breath is watching it ascend the heavens. And soon the Hound clans will gather again in their thousands at Marmalade Mountain and—'

'—and they will die in their thousands! And their blood will soak the fields of barley-weed! And Marmalade Mountain will be their tombstone!'

The Baron and Bronson whirled round angrily to see who had spoken.

It was Celia.

The Baron, seeing a Feline atop his Houndish battlements, gave a throttled cry of alarm, reaching for a non-existent sword with which to do battle. Bronson stepped between them.

'Steady, Baron! I know her.'

'Know her?' the Baron bellowed.

'Know her *and* trust her. She is Celia… Ruddegan's granddaughter.'

'Ruddegan?' howled the Baron. 'Holy snout, Bronson, how can you trust the spawn of such a devil?'

Bronson ignored the Baron. He stared into Celia's eyes, saw the fear that clouded them, saw the brimming tears.

'Why are you here, Celia? Is it Lonely you are looking for?' he asked gently.

She stared back, the tears overflowing, and with a great sob she cried, 'I have already found Lonely – and lost him. He has gone and I don't know where.'

The Baron, taken aback by her outburst, exclaimed gruffly, 'Lost, found, lost again? She's talking in riddles, Bronson.'

Bronson wiped Celia's tears with his hand, bidding her to sit. Celia slumped to the ground, her back against the battlements, exhausted, quivering.

'Best you tell us everything, Celia,' he said, squatting down beside her, his bulky frame shading her from the moon's bright light.

Her story poured from her like a river in flood. When she finished, there was silence. Finally the Baron, who had been standing bolt upright throughout, let out a primeval wail, like the first compress of a bagpipe, and collapsed to the ground.

'Rolph? Rolph?' he cried over and over again, clutching his heart as if in great pain.

Bronson too was stunned. He struggled to his feet, clutching the battlements for support. The revelation of the depths of Rolph's betrayal had rocked him to his core. So too had the shock discovery of Lonely's parentage and the cruel subterfuge that followed. Yet it was not these that caused his mighty fists to knot in anger. He turned back to Celia, and to the Baron, still moaning with hurt.

'On your feet, Baron!' he commanded. 'We have the entire Felinean army about to gatecrash our Blue Moon party. And I hate gatecrashers. Let's gather the Howlers. We can be ready to ride at dawn.'

The Baron pushed himself upright, composed himself, and stood to rigid military attention. 'And I shall rally my glorious Houndsford Motor-ized Tricycle Battalion!' he cried with new-found vigour. 'And we shall once again push these mongrel Cats back into the sea!'

The Baron had always prided himself on being ready for just such an occasion. For years, his heated warnings that 'Mark my words, the Felineans will one day rise again' had gone largely unheard. Most of the town viewed him as a lunatic old-timer with a penchant for harbouring homeless bikers. The Baron saw the Howlers as his personal army, ready to defend the nation at a moment's notice. A large number of them were housed in the ancient stables at Beaconsfield. Here, along with the Baron's huge collection of vintage military tricycles, was the Howlers' workshop, fully equipped for the endless welding, repairing and tricking up of their notorious bikes.

Celia spoke up. 'You will need much more than the Howlers or the Houndsfords to stop the Felineans!'

The Baron gave her an indignant look. 'Then what do you propose, young Celia?'

She eyed both Hounds earnestly and replied, 'You need Lonely Dog! But I don't know where to find him.'

There was a moment of silence, then suddenly, explosively, Bronson grabbed her by the arm and propelled her down the spiral stairwell.

'I know exactly where he'll be!'

Houndside lay dead and silent under the curfew, except for the unaccustomed sound of jazz music crackling from a lone radio and spilling out into the cold night air. The solitary Tom Cat in the dimly lit guardhouse was bent over it, straining to hear. A naked bulb dangled above him and a small wood-burner in the corner belched more smoke than heat.

Lonely prised the barbed-wire fence open and squeezed through.

The Tom looked up, peering into the blue-tinged darkness.

Of all the jobs to pull, this had to be the worst. Stuck in a miserable wooden shed, ostensibly guarding… what? A derelict Hound orphanage. All the action was happening down in the Port! Something big was up: the dim-witted Hounds were about to be dealt with once and for all – finally! And here he was, sitting on his icy butt up Tumbleton Avenue, protecting a disused dog pound.

Lonely froze.

The Tom, seeing nothing, turned back to the radio.

The Houndside Orphanage did not so much sag on its crumbled foundations as slump completely comatose. The rows of windows now resembled a pirate's smile – black and empty. The front door swung listlessly on its rusted hinges and the hallway floorboards were so rotten that the basement was clearly visible below. Rats peered up malevolently from the darkness.

Lonely made his way cautiously along corridors that thronged with memories. Curtains of cobwebs entangled his snout and more than once his foot plunged through the decaying floor with a sickening crack.

He was moving as if in a dream and voices from his past wafted around him like ghosts. He was not sure what he was looking for or even why he'd felt compelled to come back.

His mind still churned from Rolph's confession. He could make no sense of it, was untouched by the emotion of it, as if he were a judge, listening impartially to the impassioned speech of the accused.

Yet there was something rising within him, welling up like a poisoned spring, filling his head, pulsating at his temples, blinding him to reason.

Anger. Unrefined, vengeful anger!

How could he have been so foolish? How had he let Flannegan deceive him so? His whole life a deception! Everything a lie!

For a long time he traipsed the empty corridors and rooms, oblivious to the ravages that wind, rain and time had wrought.

Suddenly he heard something. The sound of someone shuffling about above his head. In the attic! Then the distinctive crackling sound of a needle being dropped on to an old record. The wind-up gramophone!

Lonely made his way up the stairs, as he had done countless times as a Houndling, to the trapdoor that opened on to the attic floor.

By now music crackled down the stairway, filling his ears with a sound and a memory that overwhelmed him.

Oh the sea is so cruel, and the wind cuts like a knife

And sweethearts and lovers they only cause strife

For only one thing is true and won't surely part

A five-string guitar and one broken heart

On the floor of the attic, hunched over the gramophone and with his back to Lonely, was Rolph Flannegan. Oblivious to Lonely's presence, he was lost in a reverie that was all consuming.

Lonely stood in the musty shadows for a long time, watching the old Headmaster, his breathing ragged, his soul ready to explode in a fit of rage. By the time the needle had slipped its last track and the attic was filled with its repetitive static, Lonely's head was thumping like a drum.

Before him was the Hound who had cheated him of his birthright, lied to and humiliated him, abandoned him to Catside, to the Shipwood Mountains, to a life always on the run. Then he had had the gall to beg forgiveness – as if it had all been simply an error of judgement! This Hound had destroyed his trust, his dreams – *his very life*!

Lonely felt his vision blur, felt a roar bellowing up from deep within.

Without turning, the old Hound suddenly spoke, causing Lonely to halt, his heartbeat erratic, his eyes wild.

'You have every reason to hate me, Lonely. Every reason. Do what you have to do. I of all Hounds understand.'

Then he bowed his head and closed his eyes, his wrinkled hands dropping into his lap.

Lonely blinked, stepped back a pace and with a shudder that shook him from head to toe, he awoke.

Awoke from his blind rage, awoke from his hate. The blood-red fury was gone. Lonely dropped to his knees and fell upon the back of the old

Hound, his grandfather, sobbing so much that a startled coven of ravens took flight from the rafters and soared into the night sky.

That is how Bronson and Celia found them a short while later.

'They've arrived!' Celia called, turning from the broken attic window.

It had been many hours since she and Bronson had discovered Lonely and Rolph. Now dawn was breaking.

Bronson joined her, staring down on to Tumbleton Avenue. An early-morning fog shrouded the overgrown Orphanage grounds, yet the sound of jackboots on the streets below was unmistakable. So was the throaty rumble of heavy machinery.

'Tanks!' Bronson cursed. 'There'll be trouble now.'

He peered down the driveway at his own entourage of three hundred Howler bikes massed in pairs like steel cavalry steeds. They had ridden all night along back roads and over remote passes to avoid the roadblocks and arrive at the Orphanage undetected. The startled night-watchman had bolted from his shed as they crashed his flimsy barbed-wire barri-cade, and had then headed off to alert the Toms.

However it wasn't the Toms' black sedans that now hove into view.

'Felineans!' Bronson hissed.

'Felinean troops!' Celia gasped. 'We've run out of time!'

She turned to Lonely. He was lost in thought, staring at a tattered magazine cover depicting a young Van Trong with his guitar slung over his shoulder. Rolph was asleep on the old couch.

'Lonely! LONELY!' she cried. He looked up, his eyes red-rimmed and distant. 'There are Felinean troops outside! You must act – *now*!'

The words echoed in his ears, as if coming from a long way off. It had been like that all night – Celia and Bronson desperately imploring him to make a move, to rally Hound and Cat beneath the Blue Moon at Marmalade Mountain. Yet he had remained impervious to their pleas. Lost in some strange landscape of his past, with no compass. They had even tried to get old Rolph to convince him, but he had simply shaken his head and receded into the shadows.

A burly Howler suddenly crashed open the attic trapdoor.

'Bronson! Those Cats have got some serious hardware! What's the plan?'

By way of answer Bronson strode across the floor and snatched the tattered magazine out of Lonely's hands, crumpling the Van Trong cover and tossing it over his shoulder. Then he thrust his face into Lonely's, snout to snout.

'He's dead, Lonely! Dead and gone! And there ain't nothing in this world gonna bring him back! At least you got the chance to find out who your father was, 'cause this place was full of guys who never did, me included! And he wasn't some whisky-soaked-loser either. He was a hero! So now Fate has given you an almighty opportunity to honour your father's memory. Arthur, it's about time you started acting like him – like Van Trong. It's time for you to be a hero!'

Lonely stared into the big Hound's eyes. Then, like a Hound who was all but drowned, he looked to the surface and with one last gasp clawed his way to the light and to the air.

'Let's go, Bronson. I'm ready!'

The Houndlings clung to Bella's apron and peered through the windows of their rooms above the curry house. The Blue Moon was still glowing magnificently even with the morning sun competing for attention. The instinctive urge to pack picnic baskets, clamber excitedly into buses and pick-ups and head north to Marmalade Mountain was thwarted by the sight of Felinean troops patrolling the Port's empty streets, enforcing the curfew.

'Will the Blue Moon Festival be cancelled?' enquired a wee Houndling with tears in his eyes.

Bella didn't answer, for she was much more concerned about the black silhouette of a Felinean battleship heaving into view around Gnarling Point.

Kelzie was twiddling the dials of the little radio on the bookshelf and suddenly a familiar voice broke through the static. It was Lonely Dog!

To those of you listening out there in Port Alveridge, in the Shipwoods, up in Freedom Swamp and Molars Post, and even in Ravensport and Narmel, this is Lonely Dog. I'm broadcasting on a portable transmitter from a place dear to my heart – the old Houndside Orphanage.

'There are those who would try to stop me broadcasting and stop you listening, those who want to tear down the radio masts, silence my voice and your voices, those who even now are preparing for war. But I'm telling you, they will not succeed!

Kelzie

As a Hound I loved, but never knew, once sang:

> So tell me, when will the wars all end?
>
> When will they lay down their guns?
>
> When will peace be the message we send?
>
> Can you tell me the answer to that my friend
>
> When will the wars all end?

Well, I've got the answer to that question! The wars will end when we all join together, and when we do there won't be any force big enough to stop us! So, I say to you, Cat and Hound, young and old, rich and poor, one and all, come make a stand beneath the Blue Moon! Come to Marmalade Mountain! Come together! Come now!

I'll see you there!

The Howlers' bikes roared to life, Bronson at the head. With a wave of his arm they thundered out of the Orphanage driveway and tore down Tumbleton Avenue, straight into a phalanx of Felinean soldiers. The Felinean soldiers were caught off guard and by the time they'd swung their lumbering tanks into position the Howlers were among them. Bronson landed a savage upper-cut on a brawny Felinean officer as he thundered by. With heavy chains whirling above their heads, the bikers cut a swathe through the stunned Felinean troopers and sped down Tumbleton Avenue in a cloud of choking exhaust fumes.

From the attic window old Rolph watched the hated Felineans regroup and give furious chase.

'Bronson will lead them Moggies on a merry chase,' he said grimly, then turned to Lonely. 'What will you do now?'

Lonely smiled. 'You mean what will we do now?'

'These old legs and leaky lungs won't make it to Marmalade Mountain – you'll have to leave me and take the back roads yourself, lad.'

Lonely shook his head. 'I already left you behind one too many times, Rolph. And anyway, whose going to ride the bike if you don't come with me?'

'Bike? What bike?'

But Lonely was already scrambling through the trapdoor.

'You still know how to jump-start your old Houndster, don't you?' he called back with a laugh. 'Because it's sitting in the woodshed waiting for some old Reveller to fire it up!'

The streets of Port Alveridge were still empty as old Rolph, hunched over the rusty handlebars, gunned his spluttering Houndster along the Boulevard. He wore cracked goggles and a maniacal grin. In the dented sidecar sat Lonely, with a grim smile and wind-blasted ears.

They roared past the Green, ringed with barbed wired and desolate. For a moment they turned to look at each other, remembering another time, another place. Then, in a cloud of fumes, they thundered north to Marmalade Mountain.

CHAPTER XXVII

From Heart-Throb to Hero

Stand tall all my brethren
Stand firm and stand proud
There's a new wind a blowin'
And its blowin' out loud
It's a bold cry of freedom
It's the power of the heart
It's the joy of deliverance
And a glorious new start.

—Freedom Hymn, *Juke Songbook, #99*

*C*yrus stood on the mammoth stone stage carved from
the rock at the foot of Marmalade Mountain. Before him,
the vast field bathed in blue was empty and quiet. He smiled
to himself: his plan had worked, no Hound had dared
break curfew and risk the journey out to this place. Those
foolish enough to try would encounter an army of Toms
with instructions to shoot first and ask questions of the dead
later. He had personally overseen the curfew, the
checkpoints, the barriers. The Powers in Felinea would
be impressed with their new Governor.

So immersed was the new Governor in these cheering thoughts that he
did not hear the sergeant running up the stone steps of the stage, did not
see him until he stood before Cyrus flushed and agitated.

'Governor! You'd best come quickly. There's been a development!'
Cyrus pushed past the sergeant and strode off the stage.

'Is it Ruddegan? I gave strict orders that he was to be held in his office until after the invasion.'

Before the sergeant could answer there was a sound in the distance, faint at first, but rising quickly until it thundered in the still night air.

'What the…?' Cyrus began to run towards the roadblock.

He did not have to wait long to find out.

Belting across the expansive barley fields that encircled Marmalade Mountain, in clouds of dust and exhaust, came the source of the thunderous noise. The Howlers. Three hundred motorbikes bearing leather-clad Hounds roared into view with a rumble of engines that would make the dead rise and block their ears.

At the gate, Cyrus and the Toms had only seconds to leap for safety as Bronson himself, leader of the pack, smashed through their wooden

Cast and Crew

beyond the hills. A noise like an earthquake. He looked up in horror.

Pouring over the ridge, spilling into every field, emerging from every valley and hilltop, from every direction, were thousands of vehicles of every description and kind, from old pick-ups to spluttering buses, seven-wheeled Trunkriders to rusty sedans, all packed to their roofs with Hounds. Cyrus's roadblocks had not stemmed the flow, only made it fan out into the surrounding fields and countryside. Mother Hounds with pups, grandfather Hounds and aunty Hounds and gypsy Hounds and worker Hounds! They flowed like an unstoppable river whose banks had broken, sweeping all before them. A torrent of Houndkind intent on getting to Marmalade Mountain.

At last they growled and sputtered to a stop, completely encircling Cyrus and his Toms, with a thousand horns blaring.

'What about my curfew?' he cried pitifully above the cacophony. 'I could have all you Hounds shot!'

Bronson looked over his shoulder and pointed. 'Maybe. But you wouldn't start shootin' your own kind now would you? Don't imagine your Felinean bosses would take too kindly to that!'

Over the brow of the hill, streaming in an interminable convoy, seeping into the meadows and over the ridges, came sleek limos, cheery red Pussingtons, and sports cars with their tops down. Jam-packed with…

'Cats!' cried Cyrus in disbelief. 'What are Cats doing here?'

'Same as us all, I guess,' Bronson replied. 'They've come to hear Lonely Dog sing.'

'Lonely Dog?' Cyrus wheeled round, his eyes wild with disbelief. 'That little mongrel is here?'

'In the very flesh,' said Bronson, pointing to the highest of the nearby hills. 'And I'd watch what you call him with so many of his Hound and Cat admirers standing by.'

Every eye turned to look. Over the hill ablaze with the last rays of the setting sun came a single flag, blood red, emblazoned with a running Hound. Then came the sound of something almost unearthly – the skirl of the pipes! Across the ridge, in rows of fifty abreast, came the Baron of Beaconsfield and his Houndsford Motorized Battalion. Riding pillion on the Baron's bike was Celia, holding on to the old soldier's blazer, smiling with delight.

The Baron signalled the convoy to a halt and the columns of vintage tricycles parted arthritically as from the rear Rolph rode to the front with Lonely in his sputtering old sidecar.

Resplendent in his trademark suit, Lonely dismounted and walked slowly, deliberately, through the serried ranks as Rolph cut the engine. The Toms nearby cocked their weapons and stared down their sights. Lonely continued walking, guitar slung across his shoulder.

Cyrus, apoplectic, stared aghast as one by one his Toms lowered their barrels, emptied their cartridges and set down their weapons. Still Lonely walked – the only moving creature in a landscape held motionless. When Lonely was fifty feet from the roadblock, Cyrus ordered the Toms to seize him. He was met by silence; they did nothing. When he was twenty feet from the barrier, Cyrus reached for his own gun to find it had vanished from his belt. Lonely got to within five feet of Cyrus, who glared down at the little Hound as though he might kill him with a stare. Arthur met the Governor's hostility with a still, calm gaze, reached for his guitar and strummed a flurry of notes by way of greeting. Cyrus flushed and looked down.

'Now if you'll excuse us, Governor,' said Bronson sarcastically, 'we have things to do – food to cook and tents to pitch, and a concert to get underway tomorrow. You're welcome to stay but I think you may have urgent business to attend to – like sending your troops home.'

'The Felinean army will bomb this festival to kingdom come!' Cyrus hissed, but his voice fractured as he said it.

Bronson grabbed the startled Governor by the collar. 'Not when you tell them that their sons and daughters are here. Get going and make the call!'

Ruddegan tried the door again, but it was securely locked. Cyrus had made sure of that. He stumbled back to his desk and in a drunken rage swept all its contents, including the cheap stogie he had been smoking, on to the carpeted floor.

On a large table in the centre of the office stood the architect's model of his dream city, Ruddegonia. Angrily, he staggered over to it, raised his fist and began to pummel the thing into matchsticks. Finally he sank exhausted to the floor, amid the ruins of his empire.

All was lost! All his dreams had become nightmares. All his plans had been dashed.

Suddenly he became aware of a sound.

He stood, shuffled through the debris and went to the window.

It was music! Music carried on the wind, from a distance, amplified and distinctive. It must be coming all the way from Marmalade Mountain!

Outside, young Felines in open-topped cruisers and convertibles clogged the streets below, Lonely's songs pumping from their car radios. The younger Cats had spread the word and en masse they were on the move to Marmalade Mountain.

Those cursed Hounds had ignored Cyrus and his roadblocks and had headed for the festival regardless, just as they always had done, just as they always would. But this time, for the first time in history, the Cats were joining them as well. He almost smiled at the thought of Cyrus defeated, but his own misery was too overwhelming. He listened to the music from the streets outside and suddenly remembered with great clarity where he had heard it before.

In his mind's eye he saw a figure in a long coat and black hat, singing in protest beneath the four brick chimneys of the Cannery. Van Trong. He had sung that same song on the night of his death. His death by my hand, thought Ruddegan, and this time a smile did creep across his old lips. At least I knew how to deal with the dogs! He recalled that night all those years ago. The fuel drums hidden under the crates upon which Van Trong sang, the explosion, the flames.

The memory was so vivid he could almost feel the intense, murderous heat.

In fact he *could* feel it! On his back!

He wheeled round in horror, and saw that his entire office was ablaze. His smouldering stogie must have ignited the matchstick ruins of Ruddegonia! He made a dash for the door, but the flames drove him back. He screeched for help, smashing his fists on the window, but his office was at the top of the Cannery, far, far above the factory floor.

And anyway, there was no one there to hear his final screams.

As the flames consumed him, A. K. Ruddegan's last view was of the four chimney towers, black against the moon, like prison bars.

And the last sound he heard was an old Van Trong song, playing in the distance:

But Boss Man you get ready 'cause here comes Judgement Day.

As Lonely prepared himself for the concert, the Blue Moon seemed to glow even more brightly. He wore a neatly pressed suit and tie and his winkle-picker shoes shone with pure joy.

The Felinean forces had turned tail and melted away the previous evening, and Cyrus had made himself scarce. Once the troops had left, an infinite stream of Felines and Hounds converged on the festival grounds from miles around. Word had it that there were even trainloads coming from Ravensport. Traffic was still backed up for miles. Even some of the soldiers had switched sides and were now merrily mixing it up in the crowds.

In front of the stage was a vast ocean of faces, Cats and Hounds inter-mingled. They shared blankets or simply sat shoulder to shoulder in the meadow, gathered near blazing campfires.

Behind, on the granite face, were stacked Juke Boxes and giant amps from the Shipwoods. A group of Howlers helped Luther arrange the oversized sound system, unravelling wires. They hooked up microphones to generators, plugged in jacks, and wheeled in even more amps from trucks that continued to arrive. The Sunshine Boys busied themselves tuning up their assortment of instruments. Bronson appeared with a cluster of five-string guitars for Lonely to choose from.

Backstage, Lonely stared anxiously from the shadows into the enormous crowd. He could see Celia there in the front, seated next to her new friends – the Baron and a posse of Howlers. She waved to Lonely, and he smiled back. Brother Jeroboam stood to one side, among a large gathering of leathered and coal-dusted Jukes. Rolph sat with Bella, who was crying a river of joyful tears, and a clutch of younger Houndlings played unaware nearby.

He noticed that even Elder Spittle and his wife and family had arrived with a group of friends. Toothless and Verna had also made it all the way from the hinterlands. Larry's truck appeared through the stage gate laden with a cargo of Cats all dressed up for the occasion. Forever the opportunist, Larry was busy making buckets of cash using his lorry as a shuttle from Catside.

Lonely found himself still looking, searching. There was someone missing. Kelzie. Surely she was somewhere in the vast mass? He saw some Hounds he recognized from the Orphanage, all grown up and hanging together like family, like an Alveridge County Orphanage reunion. Wouldn't she be with them? Maybe he wouldn't recognize her. Maybe she was just shy and keeping herself hidden in the throng.

As the sun sank, the glow of fires lit the upturned faces. Lonely panned the crowd again and again. An expectant hush came over his fans, all eyes turned towards the empty stage. They knew the time had come.

Bronson sidled up to the little Hound. 'You okay, Lonely? Time to sort your five-string, the Sunshine Boys are ready to roll.'

At that very moment Lonely's anxiously scanning eyes noticed a petite Houndette gently pushing through the crowd towards the stage. His heart raced. It was Kelzie, more beautiful than he could ever imagine, wearing an indigo dress and braided ears. She caught sight of Lonely standing at the rear of the stage and called out in a voice that was barely audible. 'Lonely, it's me, Kelzie! You kept your promise!' She blew him a kiss and seemed to melt into the audience of well-wishers.

Lonely turned to Bronson, beaming, stunned, feeling as if he had been woken from a dream. He said nothing, grabbed his guitar and then stepped forward into the spotlight.

Lonely had a job to do. A debt to repay. A memory to honour. It was he who had called this great throng together, and now he must do what he would always do, do what his father would do.

He stepped up to the microphone, tethered his guitar into position and said, in a voice filled with pride and power:

'Good evening! My name is Lonely Dog!'

The crowd rose to their feet and roared in jubilation.

He paused until they finally hushed. Then, in a voice charged with emotion, he continued.

'I want to dedicate this song to one who inspired me greatly, my mentor, my headmaster and my grandfather. Rolph Flannegan.'

The crowd erupted in loud applause.

Rolph gulped as his heart skipped a beat, searching for a way to vanish into the crowd. Bella's expression slowly changed from bewilderment to a glowing pride as a realization came over her. She stepped up to him and hugged him reassuringly. Rolph, once remembered as staunch, dignified and always in charge, was now an old stooped Hound with overflowing eyes, overwhelmed with emotion.

Lonely went on. 'I used to listen to him play, and his songs will always be with me.' He paused. And then, almost intimately, he said, 'Grandfather, this one's for you!'

Lonely paused. And then began to play as the light of the Blue Moon embraced him.

Port Alveridge — The Golden Years

'Alveridge 500' Street Race

The Russock Run

Cruisin' with the Houndettes

Camaraderie and Trickery!

Acknowledgements

Ivan Clarke – Lonely Dog creator, author and artist

Ivan resides near Queenstown in the picturesque Southern Lakes region of the South Island of New Zealand. He is well known for his powerful paintings of 'Middle-earth', the southern wilderness and majestic landscape of New Zealand. In more recent years Ivan has become known as the creative mind behind the fantastical world of the Lonely Dog. His whimsical paintings and drawings, known as the Lonely Dog Legacy Art Collection, have a significant following of art collectors from around the world.

As kids, Stu and I spent several summer holidays together. I remember wrecking a small rowboat attempting to surf large waves: Stu was a useless skipper and I barely escaped drowning. We would return home to the pirate camp in the backyard of our beach cottage to torment the imaginations of small boys at bedtime. There was always an abundance of tales of smugglers that would come for us in the night.

That was the age of the astronaut and bicycles with dangerously long handlebars, before sunscreen and seatbelts, or at least before anyone seemed to use them. Only the wealthy had colour TV. But we could fly. At a moment's notice we could transform ourselves into a squadron of fighter-jets, barefoot, out-running the speed of sound in the playground, trailing our arms behind us.

Sharing in the same schoolboy pranks, no doubt, left Stu and I emerging into adult life with more than a whipping from the headmaster in common. Our imaginations, some would say, thrived. Stu was always the comedian, the actor and storyteller. When I looked Stu up and rediscovered him later in life I was met with the same old grin but also with the slightly weathered look of a veteran storyteller that you don't mess with. He was the man to help me write my story, to pen the complex fantasy world into words that would appeal to more than just children. Yes, I can write too, but Stu has the edge.

What was first my story soon became our story. Stu got it immediately. It was like he somehow already knew the same wild characters and the back alleys of downtown Port Alveridge as I did. It was like he had already met the Hounds of Alveridge that, until then, existed only in my imagination and in my paintings and drawings. I guess we'd known many of these characters as lads. We discovered some things so wild and funny we couldn't print them. Now Stu has a reputation for spellbinding six hundred adolescents in a school hall with nothing but a ripping good yarn – and he gets paid for it. Cheers to Stu.

Graham Burt is also a man of great heart and talent. He is the minder and keeper of all things cool – a writer, poet, musician and friend whose creative mind is as sharp as a tack. Graham has assisted in directing the *Alveridgea* project from the early days.

He is the creative genius behind the multi-award-winning limited edition Lonely Dog book, *The Almalogue*. This celebrated, large leather-bound book – containing the original Lonely Dog story, character biographies, colour plates of my paintings, doodling and scrawling – was created as a work of art in itself and has captured the imaginations of many others who are traveling with us on this journey.

To family, friends, fans and Lonely Dog art collectors from over thirty countries around the world – thanks so much for your support.

Last but not least, I'd like to acknowledge my wife Kerry for her unwavering support and belief in me. It doesn't seem that long ago that Kerry, with our three teenage kids Michael, Raquel and Evan, said something like, 'This is cool – keep going!' I then packed up and moved over to the eccentric world of *Alveridgea*. Some wonder if I'll ever come back.

Stu Duval – Lonely Dog author, writer and storyteller

Stu resides with his wife and two boys on the Hibiscus Coast, north of Auckland. He is the author of numerous children's books and a professional storyteller, traveling the length and breadth of his native New Zealand sharing his handcrafted tales.

I wish to profusely thank the following people: Lynette, Pierre and Louis – for all the time locked away in my study hunched over this story. To Graham Burt – for laughter, headbuttings and a steady hand on this project.

And of course to Ivan Clarke – boyhood companion, raconteur and possum hunter supreme! We told many tales, swapped all sorts of lies, young sunburned, skinny lads. Now, with wrinkles and mortgages, we still tell tales and swap lies…they just get published! Thanks for the orphan dog, I know your Dad is smiling.

Graham Burt – Creative Director

Graham's background is with advertising agencies, where he represented a number of New Zealand's largest and most high-profile clients, developing products and brands for the worldwide market. Latterly he has partnered with talented Queenstown artist Ivan Clarke to develop Ivan's Lonely Dog creation, taking it to the world stage by developing the Lonely Dog brand, packaging the intellectual property and subsequently selling worldwide publishing and negotiating movie rights.

I wish to thank Jayne, Harrison and Sutherland for the inspiration and joy they bring daily. To Garry Phipps for his wise and divinely inspired counsel. To Stu for his endless creative energy and passion. And of course Ivan Clarke, the original hound himself!

Visit the official homepage of
Lonely Dog - You will
find a treasure-trove of
collectable, limited edition art,
artefacts, memorabilia and
all things Alveridgean.

www.LonelyDog.com